I0580262

Jimmy Jazz **III** Complete Works

1 House of the Unwed Mother

2 The Cadillac Tramps

3 The Sub

4 M-Theory

5 Rube Goldberg Suicide Machine

6 Where Life is Inappropriate

7 Home Despot

8 Nothing a Fire Can't Fix

9 This Ragged Muscle

10 The Book of Books

WHERE LIFE IS INAPPROPRIATE

A NOVEL BY JIMMY JAZZ

©2024 by Jimmy Jazz

First Edition

Inside-out Love Story, I am the Cancer & Is 74 Old Enough? appeared in Nothing a Fire Can't Fix 2022

The Bums Are at the Beach appeared in Sunshine Noir 2005

Red Light District, Opium Den Party appeared in What the Fuck 2000

A version of this novel appeared as a chapbook 2004

ISBN: 978-1-7358686-6-0

Book Design: Jimmy Jazz

Garamond 3, Avenir & **American Typewriter** were used in the design of this book.

Pirate Enclave Books

https://pirateenclave.square.site

Where Life is Inappropriate ⫽ a Novel

I'm an American artist and I have no guilt.

Patti Smith

The fact that certain members of the oppressor class join the oppressed in their struggle for liberation, thus moving from one pole of the contradiction to the other... Theirs is a fundamental role, and has been throughout the history of this struggle. It happens, however, that as they cease to be exploiters or indifferent spectators or simply the heirs of exploitation and move to the side of the exploited, they almost always bring with them the marks of their origin: their prejudices and their deformations.

Paulo Freire

The basic impasse of all control machines is this:
control needs time in which to exercise control.

William Burroughs

Part I: Where Life Is Inappropriate

Raise the Black Flag

I'm looking for a soft pair of lips on a determined face well read in Nietzsche. I'm suffering a peculiar primate affliction, that insatiable bonobo itch, a craving… for…

I'm sitting in the Ground Zero Café pondering the come and go, thinking about consumption, taking note of the inveterate rituals of the consumers. In this epoch, consumption defines citizenship. One of the workers has been tasked to spray down and wipe clean the tables. He smears the filth around the surface of the wood like an automaton. We don't call them retards any more. Short of getting to know him personally, we currently say he has special needs or faces a challenge from a specific affliction, fetal alcohol or Down syndrome. I don't know if Marx has anything to say about him as a worker. But he eats—in earnest by his girth. Someone with no concern for fashion buys clothes for him and he must rent a room somewhere. He's a consumer and therefore valuable.

A woman drags her ass to the counter, scratches herself and orders a large coffee. About thirty-five years of age, though most people over thirty look like generic adults to me. She has tucked a neatly folded number of the New York Times under her armpit in such a way anyone paying attention can see she reads, "The New York Times." People fly all manner of flags to broadcast their values. In front of her, a gentle man entreats the barista to offer his dog a treat from the glass jar on the counter. By gentle, I mean to describe his careful gestures, the clothing he chose and the fastidious maintenance of his ensemble. The barista wipes her hands on a dirty apron, unscrews the lid and fetches a biscuit.

"No, not that one, it's broken. And I'll have the usual."

This kind of dog is called Pomeranian. The way it sits up and begs reminds me of myself. Moved by an irresistible impulse to kick the woe gaunt brute like a football across the room, I struggle against the urge. People these days believe their dogs are human children and dote on them for reciprocation of love—and (like many parents) reinforce behavior better quashed. The barista pulls the shots and steams milk for a latte, while the dog crunches the biscuit. It licks the floor for every crumb. I don't hate animals, just some animals. The old hippie owner comes in through the back. He greets the woman and the man with the dog. His long hair has turned gray and thinned to bald at the top. He greets the dog and chucks its chin. The replies from the woman and the man with the dog sound overly familiar and border a fawning sycophancy. Because they are consumers, they are valuable. Because they are valuable, they feel entitled. The man with the dog reaches behind the counter and picks up a can of whip cream, helping himself. This chafes my sense of democracy.

Dug dug dug dug. Out front, a young mod pulls a Lambretta scooter onto the sidewalk and kills the engine. She pulls her head from the helmet and shakes her close-cut hair free. She wears dark blue jeans pegged tight at the ankle, revealing a line of skin above each desert boot, with a hint of a brown sock in the same palette as her dark green sweater. A badge near the collar reads—The Jam. Her face, the stunning youth of it, a celestial sensation—Seberg, Sedgwick, a famous face to grasp, but our young mod is undiscovered, fresh, new, exciting.

She smiles without showing her teeth as she walks into the café. Since strangers who point out my "pretty eyes" irk me, I refrain from complimenting her lips. How stupid it sounds in my head—Ah, I love the shape of your lips. It sounds so big-bad-wolf. So wolf-whistle. So moronically taboo.

Desire reigned-in, limited by "Propriety." I'm subject to it with the disdain a child might offer a buggering priest. I understand that I must share the air with other breathers and that we collectively decide the limits of appropriate behavior. Ah, since you like my eyes and I fancy your mournful lips, a kiss as you fly by may suit our needs… I'm a lip reader. Tipped off by a subtle distinction of the mouth, a quality. The texture, hue and shape tell me how far a girl will go, what she will and won't. I met a fellatio artist once, a bona fide maestro, a real PhD of the craft who all but sucked these eyes through the head of my cock. Her muscular lips told the story of her life.

I'm hopped up on caffeine, a jitterbug, so high and scattered I lose interest. Already this desire, beaten into a hunker, has limped away.

You think you know what you want, but it turns out to be somethin' else.

Alias Jimmy Jazz—poet, alias Johnny Handcock—bad check writer, alias Teddy Trask—slip and fall man, alias Stiv Snatch—debt collector. I've squandered a dozen names signing up to win things I don't need—ac, cd, pc, tv, vc—I once worked as a bounty hunter and got paid to track one of my aliases.

On Saturdays, I think. My thoughts shout at each other like an old married couple, I CAN THINK WHAT I WANT.

During the week, the public entrusts me with their adolescent children: wild offspring of animal parents, feral-brained mad girls and baby anarchists. So, I contend with responsibilities and expectations. Rules of order and decorum. The Principal wishes I shared more of his principles. In Washington, teachers can't wear disguises in public; in Tennessee, they can't talk about kissing; in the old days, teachers couldn't dance in public, drink, smoke, marry, bob their hair, get a shave in a barber shop or espouse communism.

Adults of my generation say they'd love a teacher like me— young, hip, alive through all my senses, a Tyger burning bright in the forest of the night. They admire the lion on the veldt coursing prey.

But teaching would cage the lion, like a puzzled panther. Teaching spreads across your skin like a banal fungus. I planned to be that cool teacher, to share my vast life experience and wow them with eclecticism. Have you heard this band, read this poem, seen this film?

Who would win in a fight between the Marquis de Sade and Leopold von Sacher-Masoch?

I wanted to construct panoramas of tunnel vision. Drop kids into the transmogrifier of my overwhelming pedagogy and shine a light on the horror of growing up.

"I'll be the nightlight against your terror."

A torpid coed looks up from her textbook. Did I utter that last bit aloud? My Ed professors warned me, "Choose a career: artist or educator." No side hustles in the game; teaching requires dedication.

The coed stares at me as if I were insane while she highlights whole paragraphs in Piaget. I read Piaget, Dewey, Gardner… But I also read Zinn, Goodman, Illich, Tobocman, *The Pedagogy of the Oppressed* and *Teenage Liberation Handbook*. I'd like to warn her off, tell her what to expect in the trenches. A smudge of pink lipstick marks the rim of a white ceramic cappuccino cup at her elbow. Her lips are hard, thin, pursed. She'll probably be a good teacher.

The system is my paycheck. Capitalism rules my service. Who am I? Danny, Dan, Daniel? Mr. Johnson, eighth grade English teacher? Or Cap'n Jazz, agent of skull control in pirate garb? A black eye patch and me flag the Stars & Stripes dyed black and repurposed with the skull & crossed bones. My country 'tis of thee, sweet land of misery…

If I tell you I'm a liar, how do you know I'm not lying? If I tell you I'm sane… Sanity is like breathing; you become aware when there's a problem. Sanity is an uncracked skull. All kidding aside, I'm not crazy—avast, but a humble schoolmaster.

Last week, I took 150 eleven-to-fourteen-year-olds camping under the stars. Purple mountains majesty. Blue-bleak faces at 3am. Exposure to a new world through exposure to the elements. Trees, beautiful green trees to breathe. Ahhh… and a raccoon sniffing around for food.

Georgie Evans, a goofy twelve-year-old, arrives at school twenty minutes late. He arrives toting his camping gear, a huge chaotic mess spilling and unfolding out of itself. We are supposed to depart on three school buses in fifteen minutes. One hundred forty-nine children on time with permission slips and one Georgie late without one.

"You are not going camping with us."

Mary O'Malley balances on a panicked nerve. She's been checking and rechecking permission slips since six this morning, in sustained exasperation. You can hear the short circuit cackle in her brain. The kids call her Mrs. Chins.

By the sleep crust in his eyes, Georgie just woke up. He seems dumbfounded at first, like a pan of water set to boil.

"Wh, wh, wh…"

These sounds, these phonemes, sub-word, which vent from his lips carry emotion to the air with droplets of spittle. The better part of his frustrated rage chokes on hyperventilation, though some spills out of his ear and eye holes. One pictures Bugs Bunny facing a bull with steaming nostrils. The arms flap like well-greased ball bearing akimbo pinwheels as tense fingers congeal into fists. His feet rock into an intensifying tantrum.

Convulsive blubbering shakes his soft body. Tears streak down smooth cheeks. He stutter-gags one word. In retrospect, the perfect word strung like a popcorn garland to culminate, ultimately, in exclamatory punctuation. The ridiculous sobs draw the word out, stretch it like taffy, giving it a sloping convulsive rhythm.

"B~~~I~~~T~~~C~~~H!"

Mrs. Chins pays no attention and crosses the room to help a bone-skinny seventh grader refold her sleeping bag by yelling.

"Roll it up and put it on the truck."

To me, under her breath she adds, "Stupid fucking kids."

Adults say they would have loved a teacher like Mrs. Chins in high school too. She sips from a coffee mug bearing the slogan:

WARNING: P-M-S B-I-T-C-H.

If called to task for his outburst, Georgie could argue he was innocently reading the cup, though he doesn't usually complete reading assignments in class. His so-busy brain works constantly under the chaos. If my thoughts yell, his are in a perpetual gunfight. He's shown gumption, though my official position lies between consternation and dismay.

"I've exhausted my patience for that permission slip."

"I... I... I brought it, Mr. J."

About this time, his sister steps into the classroom behind him and drifts momentarily to her own time at school here. She sat in the back by the window, passed notes to a friend. A boy she liked never saw her.

"Georgie. Georgie."

"Ya, Mr. J."

"I can't believe I'm taking you to the wilderness."

His face brightens as he turns around. His sister may be a hundred pounds overweight—carried in her ass, upper arms and face. She clutches a Burger King sack in one hand and the permission slip in the other. Georgie's nephew plays with a toy car on the floor in her shadow.

The bulk of students wait in lines, anxious, excited, yet cool. Puffy Oakland Raiders jackets and Yankee baseball caps turned brim back. Some of the boys wear knitted wharf caps pulled low on their foreheads. Georgie stands taller in line than most and looks awkward.

The other teachers transcend chaos. At least, you can't see any outward effect. They chose to expose these kids to the wild—assessed a need and stepped to meet it. Our imperious leader, the Principal, says things like, "Measure the weight and gravity of responsibility against your experience and character and go forth undaunted." The school's mission, after all, requires us to expand the possibilities of our students.

Nine parents marshaled the temerity to sally forth into the mountain with us. I don't expect much help. One of them has a different notion about camping—behind the wheel of an rv, with a bed, tv, kitchen, shower and satellite dish. One of the parents left the comfort of home because of the campground's proximity to a casino. B-I-N-G-O and video slots are her games, Oh.

Sneaky

"Rosendo, would you sit down, sit. I need to talk to you."

The other kids went home. The clock on the classroom wall reads 4pm. This is the first classroom I've been allowed to decorate—I brought in a painting by my friend, the artist SF McBean and some posters that hung in the room where I lived in college. The kids don't ask why Billy Idol screams Generation X. They don't care about Hüsker Dü or Black Flag.

I'm sitting on my desk watching this young man circle the room. His sticky fingers pick up a wooden ruler, which has been school property since 1957. He's twiddling it and I can hear my mother say, "Danny, stop fidgeting." Since she said it around four thousand times, I don't bother. Without warning, his body settles into a student desk. His left leg kicks air. Postures can say nervous, scared, lying, excited. His shouts "Fuck You" at the world and at me in particular. His hands twist over the ruler. In the 1950s, he could have marched before the band.

"Rosendo, at this school we practice respect for the rights of others to learn and study."

His knees jiggle under the desktop.

"Respeto a los derechos ajenos es la paz."

"I didn't do nothing."

I can hear Keith Morris, lead singer from Circle Jerks, screaming, *Deny everything... Deny everything.* The tone of Rosendo's voice projects what my mom identified in me as "Angst," anger cut with anxiety. SF McBean and I drove up the I-5 to see Circle Jerks in Long Beach a few years ago. I shaved half my head—hippie from the left, skinhead from the right—which meant that I had to be hyper-vigilant against Nazis grabbing me by the hair or anarcho-punks punching me for a Nazi. After the show, a pack of skins brandished snapped-off car antennas and chased a hippie across the parking lot.

And we're running down the backstreets Oi! Oi! Oi!.

"Don't bullshit me. You walked around the room, doing laps, poked every other kid with your pencil. You talked to Hector while I gave directions; you didn't even start the assignment. You broke all the…"

SNAP. He breaks the ruler like one of the classroom rules with ease and disregard. I was saving the "Show Respect for Property" speech for another day—he'd scribbled on a kid's paper, stole a bag of chips from Philip and a mechanical pencil from Roger. He scrawled "VELS" on the desk. To waste words on deaf ears. Actually, I had his ears tested and they worked unless he found a way to cheat on the hearing test. The brain transcribing the sound waves follows its own agenda.

I'm calm, unshaken by the destruction of the ruler. Rosendo lets the broken pieces fall to the floor. The wood CLATTERS on the tile and falls silent.

"What's going on with you, man?"

I would add, "What kind of drugs are you on?" but we aren't allowed to ask. The school doesn't want to be sued for libel. So, we assume they are high as kites. As an adult, I can't tell. I've known users: roommates, family, friends. One idiot roommate in college invited some chemistry geeks to set up a meth lab in the garage. Maybe Rosendo's one of those crack babies the news reported. His mom looks like she sniffs glue or eats pills. One of those LSD test pilots. I don't know. I don't care; I do care. Comparing the genetic structure of crack cocaine with Rosendo's DNA yields a 99% match. He's wasted in the most basic physiological sense.

"Hello, Mrs. Juarez, Mr. Johnson here, from Ed Abbey Middle."

"Ho-la, Mee-ster. Yon-son."

"Rosendo got into another fight today. That means suspension."

"Can you keep him with you? Please, Mr. Yonson. Don't send him home."

The next day, Rosendo sneaks into class after the bell.

"Rosendo's late, you should mark him tardy, Mr. J."

"That's funny, Khahn."

Khahn Nguyen comes in late most days. Rosendo whispers in his ear and Khahn gives him a shove. Rosendo stumbles back but springs forward and slaps Khahn on the arm. When Khahn pushes himself up from the desk, he stands about six inches taller. Rosendo squirms away like jooking a tackle, but Khahn's fist THUMPS him on the shoulder blade.

"Ooooo."

I remember getting punched in seventh grade; I remember how much it hurt. Rosendo doesn't cry, but wants to. He stares at Khahn like he'd kill him if he could.

I'm already in between them and warding off repercussions from cousins and older brothers. The class voted Rosendo most likely to provoke a race riot.

"He asked for it, Mr. J. He said my mother sucks cocks."

Cue the rising clamor from the laugh track of a bad situation comedy. The school board should slap a Parental Guidance warning on school for explicit language and violence.

"Hello, Mrs. Juarez. We've had some problems with Rosendo-"

"He's not here. Sometimes, I no see him for days."

It's 9pm. Why am I working so late?

"I can't talk right now. My oldest boy needs to eat."

Her oldest son was shot, again, this time by a cop. He's the good son now. Reformed. He loves his mother. One of the other teachers told me all this. Teachers indulge in gossip as much as anybody. The police pulled the car over after the driver rolled through a stop sign. Four homies in a 69 Impala, the cop said he saw a gun. One boy was killed, Rosendo's brother took a slug in the leg.

"Hey, Rosendo, how do you feel about what happened to your brother?"

He doesn't answer. He'd been jumped into this life against his will.

"Rosendo told me he went to school today, Mr. Yonson. He said you were a bad teacher. He said it was boring, especially your class. He says he wants to go to a different school. He said Abbey School has bad policies."

At home, I flip through an old psychology textbook. I didn't tell Mrs. Juarez that Rosendo has a self-esteem problem; I don't know what to tell her.

Rosendo arrived at school, tardy, the next day with a dirty face, like his mom or older brother had dragged him through the mud. Cheekbone darkened by a blue-black bruise.

"Hey, who gave you the shiner?"

"I fell off my bike."

"Ouch. My best black eye came from beach volleyball, summer of 1982, you were born…"

He's stopped listening, but I continue.

"This hypercompetitive lout we used to play with, an oafish character overestimating his aptitude without the slightest concept of teamwork, clocked me with his elbow as we dove for the ball."

Initially, the blue-black bruise sat above the eye, under the brow, but the dead blood fell in a clump and sat for weeks. I made up a story every time someone asked. Told my teacher I was hit with a baseball; told my friend Roy my girlfriend punched me; told my girlfriend Roy shot me with a BB gun; told my mom I fell on the stairs…

"I fell off my bike."

Rosendo's cumulative file notes a series of bike accidents beginning in the fourth grade. His second-grade teacher suspected he was a pathological liar and referred him for counseling. His crippled brother probably knocked him around at his mother's behest.

"What happened to your eye, Rosendo?"

"I fell off my bike."

"Yeah, right, you know your mama beat you down."

Khahn laughs and the laugh track follows on cue. My textbook says, "Teenagers may laugh to hide discomfort."

"Rosendo, take a seat."

Bloodshot red tendrils grow on his eyeballs like red ivy on a white wall. So red that little white shows. He might be stoned. No pencil, no notebook. I give him a new notebook with "LOANER" stenciled across the front. It comes with a free pencil. It's the third day of school. Later that day, he gets sent out of math class unable to focus. He's already lost the loaner notebook.

I give him a Reflection Sheet to analyze the events that got him kicked out of class, gain awareness of his actions and develop a superego—a time killing machine in his case—but he's already talking to Pepito Escobar, who should be reading about Pancho Villa.

"Okay... outside."

I escort Rosendo out by the arm, but he scoots away. His sneakers skitter on the floor as he dodges me. The entire class looks up from reading. I feel like a sheep dog, a sheepish sheepdog, as I herd this kid toward the door.

"Hey, man, I'm not going to spend this whole year babysitting you."

He's sitting on a chain suspended between steel posts that separate the walkway from a planter full of shrubs. His legs swing free of the ground. A fall could crack his skull. He seems incapable of stillness.

"You'll have to serve detention after school today."

He doesn't seem to hear and doesn't show up after school.

The next day, he ditches class. Joe, the School Security guard, brings him to my room.

"Sup, Mr. J. I found laughing boy hiding in the girl's bathroom."

The guard stands wider across than Rosendo stands tall. We're both in his shadow. He played football in college until his knee went out. That's his story. He has rapport with the kids, but I can't say if it's fear or respect. Rosendo thinks being caught in the girls' restroom is funny. His teeth are crooked. He doesn't laugh out loud, but the humor registers in his face.

"A girl was in there with him. She had a pass, so I sent her to class. I don't know what they were up to."

Trading makeup secrets, I want to say but don't.

"More detention?"

"I hate typing, the teacher's a little bitch."

The security guard gives him a stern look and offers me one that implies—can't argue there.

By holding Rosendo in detention, I punish myself.

"The class is boring. We don't learn nothing."

This puts us in a tight spot. Joe, the Security Guard and I know for a fact the typing teacher is totally uptight.

"What were you doing in the girls' bathroom?"

"Hiding."

"You can do your typing today after school. Tomorrow, you need to go to the class. There are ways to change your schedule. Truancy is not the way."

The next day, I'm at the Juarez home with Peter Blythe, PE teacher and tenor in a men's choir. Peter serves as spiritual mentor, physical support and guide to young teachers. As a teacher, he commands respect and models it for the children. He enjoys working out, his muscles exude fitness. Rosendo lives down the hill from the school. We drive on 61st Street in Mr. Blythe's powder blue Suzuki Samurai. He parallel parks across from the address between a 64 Chevy Malibu with carpet on the dashboard and a gray lowrider sedan.

A couple of vatos stare at us. The shorter one cocks his eyebrow at us. I'm tempted to say, "What chu lookin' at?" but it's their neighborhood. The tall fat one isn't wearing a shirt and has "East Side" tattooed on his stomach in gothic letters. A black bandanna covers his head.

"Good afternoon, boys. How are you on this fine day?"

The gimpy one on crutches must be Rosendo's older brother. Same mouth, nose, eyebrows.

"I'm Mr. B and this is Mr. J. We're Rosendo's teachers from the Ed Abbey middle school."

The gimp looks at us through one eye and wheels around on the crutches.

"You look too young to be a teacher. I've been telling that kid, but he don't listen."

Rosendo's brother leans on one crutch as he unlocks the iron security gate. Rosendo's younger brother pedals a tricycle in furious circles. Other kids laugh and play. The gimpy older brother has a white bag with red KFC lettering tucked under his arm. The smell of fried chicken grabs the little brother's attention.

"Ernie, come eat."

The matriarch sits on the couch watching a telenovela. She wears a loose T-shirt, but I can't quite read the tattooed word above her breast. The apartment looks clean. Fresh vacuum tracks mark the carpet. The furniture is worn, but functional. The mother arranged the decorous crap on the shelves near the tv with some care.

"That's a great picture of Rosendo."

There are framed photographs of all three boys on the walls.

"Mrs. Juarez, we came to discuss Rosendo's behavior."

"Yeah, I know, he no listen. He no come home from the school right now. Sometimes he no come home. I look for him at his friend's house. He no tell me where he go."

"We need you to come to the school and spend a day with him in his classes."

She looks at me like I'm deranged. It's the same stare the torpid coed gave me at the café. She adjusts her position on the couch, adjusting her shirt.

"Rosendo may not return to school until you come with him."

Peter sounds friendly, yet stern. I can see Mrs. Juarez never liked school herself. Her eyes weigh the alternatives on the fulcrum of her mind. The threat of Rosendo spending a lot of time at home washes over her face. Ernie sits at the kitchenette, tears open the KFC bag. The sound of paper RIPPING seems absurdly drawn out.

"Okay."

There's one feature of each son in Mrs. Juarez's face. She has her little boy's hope around the lips, her oldest boy's worried brow and Rosendo's loathing of school built into her bone structure. The next day, Rosendo doesn't show up.

"Mr. Yonson, Rosendo, he stayed out all night. He come in at nine this morning. He was too tired for school."

"Did he say where he was?"

"No. He would not tell me. Can you tell the office he was sick today, so I no have to call?"

I imagine telling the lady in the attendance office, "Please excuse Rosendo. He will miss class because he partied all night." This reminds me of the time I fell asleep on the sidewalk outside Helga's house without a shirt. Stinging ants crawled over me. A cat sniffed to see if I was dead.

"Class. Meet Mrs. Juarez. She will shadow Rosendo today."

She squeezes into a student desk next to her son. Looks like she ironed her clothes for a job interview. Got her hair done. The dry weather shows on her lips under a thin layer of red lipstick.

"Why is she here?"

Rosendo sneers at the speaker, says nothing.

"She wants to see the learning that goes on at Edward P. Abbey."

"She's here because Sneaky got caught smoking pot."

For most of the day, Rosendo acts like a normal student. He doesn't talk about his cock in Spanish. He doesn't harass the girls or extort money from anyone. The usual flurry of reports about ripped-in-half assignments and stolen pencils doesn't materialize. The school should pay his mom to sit with him every day.

At 1:05, I've got a prep period, so peek into Rosendo's social studies class. Mrs. Chins is running a Socratic seminar. The kids read about the deleterious influence of the Barbie doll on self-worth and have circled their desks to respond to questions.

Mrs. Chins spots me at the door.

"He actually read the story. All it took was his mother looking over his shoulder."

Mrs. Juarez sits in one of the wrap-around student desks in the circle. A traveler lost in the fog.

"Rosendo, why does the author think Barbie is bad for young girls?"

He looks at his mom. He looks at the other kids.

"Because they'll never grow boobs like hers."

"Good. Why not?"

"Rosendo, stop wiggling around."

His mother sounds like mine. The half of his body slouched above the desk remains still while his feet under the desk pedal like he's on a bike. He rides ten miles. If we harnessed that energy, installed a treadmill or issued giant rat exercise wheels instead of desks, we could light the entire school.

Mrs. Chins pokes her head into my classroom before my next class and says, "F.A. did pretty good with his mom holding his hand."

She started calling him F.A. after he wrote "Fucker Asshole" on the wall during lunch detention.

"He has typing next. He hasn't made it through a period yet this year."

"That teacher's a dumbass… hee hee. I'd like to watch the little shit eat her alive."

In the middle of the period, the typing teacher calls me over to her room. Mrs. Chins watches my class while I investigate. Students peck at the keys in every desk. Rosendo's mother occupies a chair at the back of the room.

The typing teacher hands me a sheet of paper covered with a solid block of curses:

> testes 1,2 mf cunt-liking fag dik chingada pervrt pinchi culo de plomo pussy mallate estupido fatso dooky cabron joto poop dike culo asshole homo sucks fart turd caca dickhed chikenshit bullshit dogshit horseshit cowshit pigshit donkeys ass sandex scrotum puta butmunch chinga tu marde stupid reterd dam twat dong shit jesus niggggr chupa me verge cum balls fagit mr prik peckerwood skanky chode necio nards lazy pig bendejo basturd crap flap dag nabbit scumbag feo dummy goddam moterfukin sun of a bich liar wetbak bich lesbo booby fatas bunghole chile tity jugz slut Balzac smegma hor pollo buns gay necedad tonto homo cans ass rimjob chester melester queer cocksukr fuck fucks fucked fucking funky fucker…

"He needs to work on spelling."

The typing teacher doesn't laugh. I've already decided to frame this one above my desk at home.

"Mr. Johnson, I value time. I'm concerned that Rosendo uses the correct fingering while typing obscenities. He only uses one finger."

"Let me guess which one."

"I'm not going to typing class no more."

"Ro-sen-do…"

His mother tries the same cocked eyebrow her eldest son used to dissect Mr. B and I in the street to no effect. She turns for help; I can't offer any.

Rosendo didn't go to typing class again.

Before school the next morning, I go to the social worker's office. Charlene hasn't had any solutions, but I need help. I lean on the service counter at the front, note the stainless-steel bell, but see her on the phone so lay off it. Charlene Hassler's tall enough to look most seventh graders in the eye and has boobs that precipitate sweat stains at the base of her bra. She has thick lips that she coats with Chapstick. The remains of a McDonald's breakfast are scattered across her desk. She sips orange soda through a straw and beckons me to enter.

"Mr. J, I want Rosendo to see this psychologist. Can you hold? The psychologist won't see the little shit because of his drug history. The marijuana. Talk to him."

She shoves the phone at me, which smells like cigarettes. The earpiece feels hot against my ear.

"Hello, sir. Yes, I'm Rosendo's teacher. You should pick him up on your…uh… caseload."

"We don't treat drug addicts, sir. The treatments aren't effective. Charlene knows that."

By the sound of his voice, I can tell that Rosendo would aggravate his ulcer.

"He's never been busted for drugs at school."

"I saw in his file."

"CPS picked him up with a bag of pot, sure, but he only stole it from his dad to embarrass the old man at work."

"Has he been evaluated for an Individual Education Plan?"

"Just a second. He wants to know about an IEP."

"He can't bill the school district unless the subject has one."

"Can we get one? How long?"

"With cooperation from Rosendo's parents, it would require a month to test and assess. Another month for an appointment."

"No, no, no. He isn't a learning-disabled case. He's a social-emotional disaster. Is that a category? He might have an attention deficit. I want to keep this kid from falling into a life of gangs and drugs. He's twelve. We all need to do what we can to pull him back from the edge. He needs someone to talk to."

"Why don't you talk to him? Fit him out with an IEP."

A bell goes off and I'm called like a fighter into the ring.

"I need to go to class now, sir, Doc, I'll start the process."

"Hmmm."

I've noticed that most of the adults and all of the kids have exhausted their patience with Rosendo. There's nothing likable about him. He exhibits rude or lewd behavior at every juncture. Someone told me that he cruises the elementary school to meet girls. He steals and lies every day. He was *born to lose and destined to fail* as the song says. I didn't expect him to slap a transfer form on my desk. I keep the yellow copy, pink for the office and the white gets jammed in his pocket. He smiles like he won some kind of prize. It's the same inappropriate grin from when he was caught in the girls' bathroom. It's the same lying smile he put on when the security guard caught him "taking a leak" behind the storage shed near the school's back gate. I've seen that obscene gesture a dozen times. It struck with solemnity that I wouldn't see it again.

"We're moving."

"Where to?"

"I ain't telling you, Johnson."

I called his mom later that day to verify the story.

"These friends get him in trouble."

Mrs. Juarez moved her sons out of the district, so Rosendo's file and case closed several days later.

Field Trip

"If they're too stupid to get on the bus, we sure as hell don't want to take them to the mountains."

Mrs. Chins cross-checks names with permission slips. Catches sight of Georgie's head at the back of the bus, mid-conversation with the girl next to him.

"What's he doing? He didn't turn in a damn permission slip."

She examines her clipboard.

"Georgie, get off of this bus. No slip, no trip."

"I do too. I do too."

"His sister brought it."

Mrs. Chins, hair awry, folds her lips into a snarl. She stares at Georgie and he stares back, as if righteous indignation were enough to keep him out of the iron maiden. Mrs. Chins points an index finger for extra emphasis.

"One screw up and your sister comes to pick you up. Understand me?"

Georgie averts his eyes and shrinks into the seat to compress his body. He mumbles and rolls his eyes. Usually, the instigator next to him would shout, "Oooo, Mrs. Chins, he called you an obstreperous cunt." The students must be anxious to give school the slip.

Mrs. Chins sits near the front of the bus which leaves one spot next to Vomit Boy. He earned his name on a bus trip to sixth grade camp even though last year, Loquesha Jones stole the show screaming, "I gotta pee." Mr. Stone ignored her until she urinated in her designer extra-baggy dark blue jeans. The wet spot cut a thin yellow line of urine through the center aisle of the bus. Loquesha hung the jeans on a tree in the campground; the sun dried them out but baked in a fetid odor.

"Loquesha, did you go to the bathroom?"

"You gonna pee your pants again, Loca?"

"Yeah, Qeesha, you better not."

"What about you, Vomit Boy?"

"You gonna barf, Laurence?"

"Any puke splash on me and I kick your ass."

Laurence folds his arms across his chest and leans forward, flushes green as nausea spirals in his glazed brown eyes.

The driver looks back.

"Everybody got a seat?"

The bus pulls onto Skyline Drive, passes a series of boarded-up row houses and the high school. We pass a church, another church, three more churches and a liquor store. We pass Cotija #8 and the trolley station. We wave goodbye to bars on windows and graffiti-covered culverts.

"Your mama's chest is so hairy that Tarzan mistook her boobs for coconuts."

Mrs. Chins likes to engage in ranking battles with students.

"Whoooop."

The bus driver turns onto the freeway and checks on the commotion in his rearview mirror.

James accepts the challenge and puffs his chest like a street rooster darting between parked cars.

"Your butt is so big that George Bush used your underwear as a parachute in World War II."

Mrs. Chins cackles.

"Whoop. Whoop."

If they drop a historical fact or current event into the mix, they earn two "whoops." Mrs. Chins has replaced the pop quiz with a debasement contest. She believes it enhances their public speaking skills and she gets a rush when they jot her cut-downs in their notebooks to use against little brothers. The contest rebuilds her composure, the frazzle wears off leaving a half-tone between exasperate and sharp delight.

The bus plods along on Interstate 8 past the last tract of houses of the sprawling suburbs. We climb the foothills at a fair pace until the bus exits at the turn off for the mountain. Laurence seems overconfident, looking at comic books with his friends. Loquesha rocks back and forth. She's either singing or struggling to hold it. As the bus undertakes the first series of curves, the students grow quiet. I feel their motion sickness. I keep one eye on Laurence and reach into my backpack. I had Caledonia copy "Vomit Boy" with a purple crayon on the side of the sack under the Southwest Airline logo. She embellished it with flowers and a smiley face.

"Cali made this for you."

"Thanks, Mr. J. I got it."

The bus sways on a curve and he snags the sack from my hand. He struggles with his innards against the temptation to throw up his supper. The bus finds a straight stretch of road and Laurence closes his eyes. He mumbles a prayer.

Loquesha sings, "Ninety-nine bottles of gin on the wall… ninety-nine bottles of gin. Come on everybody."

"Shut up, Loquesha, you crazy."

We pass a stand of oak trees on the right. On the left, the first ponderosa pine alludes to the change in altitude. Mrs. Chins stares out the window and plots her next rank.

Dead Squirrel

The crisp mountain air oxidizes some of Mary Chins O'Malley's nervous energy. In a classroom, she stands like an ogre over her students. She intimidates them with the spiked cudgel of her personality. But the trees—cedar, sugar pine, ponderosa and black oak—reduce her to merely human. They tower over us and in their scale we find a reckoning of our true place in the universe. Calm, small and insignificant.

"Attention. Attention. Please be advised. My group needs to meet at the picnic tables under the oak tree."

"Which one's the oak tree?"

Mr. Blythe, Mr. Stone and Mrs. Kasunic lead their groups to various staging areas. Mistletoe grows in the branches near the top of one tree. For most of these kids, the thought of touching their lips to another seems gross. Wild Mary O'Malley, in her younger days, fastened a sprig of mistletoe to her flaming red hair and collected kisses at the staff Xmas party. "Smooches under the parasite, anyone?" That was the year that the Principal rolled dice for shots of tequila.

Mrs. Chins likes to use her lips as a weapon. "You behave, Bobby Brown, or I'm gonna give you a great big kiss." She gets away with behavior that I can't even make jokes about. The Principal would fire me as fast as he could sign the pink slip.

"When we gonna eat?"

Korrey wishes his grandma's kitchen would appear in the glade with barbecue and potato salad. He wants to play professional basketball in the football off-season. The girls love Korrey. A naiveté in his cheeks seems to say that he hasn't quite realized this. When Kandy Roberts declared him her man and beat a girl's ass to defend her stake, he didn't know what to do with her.

"You stop playing around with those little boyz, you're with me now."

I heard through channels that she went to give him head, but discovered his pubic hair hadn't grown in yet. Physical, bodily fear kept him from breaking with her. People said she slashed a girl's face with a razor in the alley. Korrey thinks of himself as a good student, though he seems to lack necessary skills—like studying. Somebody told him to consider college ball, but he gets distracted and plays around. He's a child you look up at to stare down.

"Oooggggghh."

"Gross."

"That's sick."

They've discovered the corpse of a squirrel squished on the asphalt parking lot.

"Did the bus kill it? That nasty."

My group circles around it like a schoolyard brawl. Khahn touches it with his shoe. It's more real than a fight. They don't catcall or egg on. The squirrel's eyes are gone. It's escaped the world's rage. A dry shard of bone pierces the hide where his neck broke.

"He's been dead longer than that."

"Oh, my god."

Loquesha steps back as a yellowjacket emerges from a dime-sized hole where the critter's penis once stood erect. The genitals have been eaten away. Most of the kids shriek and widen the circle.

"Is this a girl squirrel?"

"How should I know? Its thingy is gone."

I hear a bit of tremulous laughter. Stepping closer, the kids lean in.

"A girl would need nipples to feed her young."

"Nice observation of detail, Arturo."

Arturo pulls his beanie a bit lower on his forehead. I'm surprised he can see anything through his dark sunglasses. Another bug pokes its head out of the hole. The meat bees move in and out of the hole, carrying the guts off to feed their young or their queen.

"When we gonna eat?"

I came up on a Saturday with the other teachers to scout the location and create a lesson plan. We decided to set up teaching stations. Stone would help the kids calculate the heights of trees; Chins planned a craft with found pinecones. Mrs. K would ask the students to observe a square meter circle and catalog any life that strayed into it. My group will write poetry. I set up my station near the corpse—the aroma of decay inspired the air. One of the kids remarks about the peaceful nature of trees—a cliché. Or maybe a mangled squirrel terrifies them less than the evening news. A dead squirrel lacks the emotional connection with a hamster or goldfish.

A boy named Daniel writes, *Bees in your eyes, bees in your neck, bees eating at you, eating the squirrel in you.*

One hundred-fifty kids trample the spent needles and fallen leaves of heavy autumn. In the night, crickets chirp as loud as traffic and unseen animals hoot like neighbors quarreling on the other side of the wall. An airplane passes overhead. The squirrel died and in us some life still remains. This matters.

Midnight

The students hear gunshots at home in their beds, almost every night. You can't hunt duck or deer in the park, so it's pretty quiet. There's a group of seventy boys bedded down in between several granite boulders. A group of seventy-five girls were directed to lay their sleeping bags in a clearing up the trail. A thick brush line cordons off the two camps. You can reach the other camp by the trail or by a detour through the pitch-dark woods. We left the parent volunteers with Mrs. Tekhne to supervise the girls' camp. All of the students are asleep or feign sleep, exhausted by a three-mile hike. Mr. Stone confiscated the flashlights after they wouldn't stop sending signals and annoying each other. He called anchoring them in their sleeping bags for fear of the dark value added.

The teachers gather over the nearly-spent fire. The embers underneath the last log could reignite with new fuel. We've got plenty of wood.

"Did you see Melody and Brittany singing around the campfire?"

Mrs. Chins holds her nose.

"Did you hear Melody and Brittany? They must have learned that song at church camp."

"They were cute. I learned that Bean Dog song in D.A.R."

"Camping brings out weird talents."

"Who gives a fuck where your dog, Garbonzo's been? Hee hee."

This from the same Mrs. Chins who called me cynical after the host of an AM talk radio show described my generation as "jaded and nihilistic."

"I value the girls' bravery to act stupid in front of their peers."

The wind shifts smoke into my face.

"See, Mary, you've modeled that."

Mr. Stone and Mrs. O'Malley met in the 60s.

"Where's Peter?"

"He's worried about the students leaving their areas. He said he was going to walk the perimeter."

"Like at the school dance, when he chastised the only couple on the floor for dancing too close."

"I like the way he clears his throat at public displays of affection."

"I figure their silliness or stupidity varies from ours by degree and awareness."

No one responds.

Mrs. Kasunic rubs her hands over the fire. She has a bachelor's degree, in science. She has blonde hair and Mrs. T said her IQ was 135. She's the most asexual person I've met—a cipher, a nonentity, a placeholder. A social-sexual stupidity. Mrs. Chins' crude, but honest silliness helps her cope with the job.

"Nobody really likes twelve-to-fourteen-year-olds. Parents complain, but middle school teachers endure until they crack or burn out."

"When you meet their parents, you understand why the kids are assholes."

I look around for one of the parents.

"I'd like to say, 'Ma'am, your son is an idiot and after meeting you, I see why.'"

Mr. Stone laughs, but maybe about a thought of his own he hasn't shared. Mrs. Kasunic has a sour face.

"Oh, where has your dog Pinto been? PLPLPPP. Hee hee hee."

I sidestep into the rising black smoke from the fire pit.

"The police used your butt to quell anti-war protests on campus."

"Whoop. Whoop."

We understand the need to expel: students, frustration, gas.

"Nighty-night."

"Don't let the scorpions bite."

The scientist parries, less amused than assured by expert knowledge of local entomology.

"Don't let the Cuyamaca Wolf Spider suck blood from your neck."

Mrs. Chins and I warm our frozen feet and asses by the fire. The embers are still glowing. I'm drifting into a reverie. The heat cooks my face as I lean closer to the fire.

FWOOSH. The fire hisses and a thick column of whitish smoke rushes up.

"Lights out."

Stone holds an empty bucket. The embers sizzle.

"Pull my finger. We were using that fire."

Stone makes me feel like a little kid. Dousing a fire where he warmed himself seems unimaginable.

Chins and I hike to the other campsite along the midnight mountain path. We make our way by starlight and the dying beams of two cheap flashlights. I can't see my hand in front of my face.

A dwindling fire still burns at the other campsite.

"Hello."

"How's it going?"

"Good."

I count six parents. There's an empty spot where a car should be, so a small group drove to the casino.

"How's junior doing in your class?"

They warned me about late night parent-teacher conferences in teacher school. I didn't believe it when they said teaching was a twenty-four-hour job. When I was a substitute, I never had this kind of responsibility. A teacher carries the fibrous mass home, beds it down and aggregates the data in dreamland.

I step away from the group, but one of the parents follows. Her daughter always tells me how pretty my eyes are.

"Mr. Johnson, you have such beautiful eyes. Can I ask a personal question? Are you married?"

She's not bad looking. Her profane lips are thick and full and she has dark, penetrating eyes. Her kid's a pain in the ass, though.

"Well… uh… basically. My girlfriend, Alaska, we're uh… domestic partners, she likes to camp, but our daughter has a touch of flu in her lungs running out her nose as snot."

"I see. How long have you been together?"

I'd like to derail the conversation before called to explain why we're not married. My head aches. No matter where I stand, the smoke blows in my face. My sleeping bag seems so far away in the other camp.

"Hey, Peter."

The parent turns to acknowledge him.

"Did you check all the sacks, Peter? Hee hee hee."

"Not yet, but I may stay up all night. None of these girls get pregnant on my watch."

"You're crazy."

"Ha ha. I haven't been crazy since 1973."

"A wild man, this one."

There's something unsettling about 150 kids sleeping. I hear one with sleep apnea snoring. The big darkness has to scare them. There's always light in the city.

Along the trail, a raccoon darts across the path on his nightly forage—his masked face reminds me of home. It moves with stealth, a burglar, on his way to steal eggs from a jay's nest, behind a log, under a bush, the little safe-cracker might gank the hot dogs in the food cooler. The inert bodies raise the earth like a hundred shallow graves in the darkness.

I slip off my shoes, one sock, then the other. A few pine needles stick to my bare feet. I usually sleep in boxer shorts or naked, so slip out of my jeans. My legs are cold. My friend Cecil dragged me to a poetry reading on Thursday night, where the poet came out naked to read from his book. It was in an art gallery. Allen Ginsberg read poems without clothes in a movie and so did Karen Finley. Maybe it's how artists free themselves. I pull off my shirt, wrap up the boxer shorts and socks and snuggle into the bag. I cram myself all the way in and cover my head to warm up. My own hot air works like a heater. Twenty people sat on the floor in the gallery. I wasn't the only one who was surprised. I'd been to strip joints and seen strippers with agate eyes disrobe, but hadn't thought about what it meant before the poet.

Another midnight might have seen me playing my favorite pinball machine at the joint on Midway Avenue near the old Naval Training Center. I sweat when I play pinball. I jump with body English to ease the ball away from the drain. There are two ways to win a free game, to gain an extension of life. Sometimes the lucky numbers match, but when the free game comes on points and you hit a high score, no sound offers more thrill than the CLOK! of victory. Pinball, a game of skill, matures with every quarter in the hole. You develop a rhythm. In a strip joint, when the ball zips down the middle between the flippers, you've lost, but a naked woman dances for survival to pop music. I had never considered what it was like to be that girl. Dirty old men lick their lips; dirty young men stuff dollar bills into elastic garters. I should have thrown a buck at the poet. Cecil and I drink whiskey from a flask in the car before we go out. We watch sailors blow their paychecks on marked-up Budweiser and girls shake their asses on stage. Losing is inevitable. It's midnight and there's less of our dead squirrel out there, ant by ant, passing through the bellies of maggots, in total darkness, and sleep spirals like a silver pinball around the black hole of a bottomless drain.

A Wet Dream

We're at the zoo, standing in front of the naked mole rat exhibit. The keepers put them in clear plastic tubes, like a hamster Habitrail, allowing us to see how they organize their society. A queen attended by drones will pee on the food supply to render her rivals infertile and fuck any of a dozen consorts according to her will. Guards, foragers, cleaners, builders. They are a hive of mammalian bees.

I am living in the naked mole rat dream.

In a mirror, squint your eyes and scrunch your chin toward your nose. My skull has been shaved like a shrunken head on a string. Furrowed and scarred brow. Buck teeth. I see myself lying dead with insects devouring me. These are forbidden thoughts.

I'm meandering through the woods. Being a mole rat hurts. The pain stalks me but I can outrun it. If I'm caught, put my skin, guts and hair in a pine box, bleach my bones and wire them together for biology class. I will finally succeed at teaching.

I go back, I go down, nothing. I don't know what's wrong. Don't know what's chasing me. You can't assume it broke until you know what it is. Maybe my disease, dormant like a herpes virus, climbs to the surface of the skin in times of stress. I'm not even a mole rat, I'm a lesion on my own skin, a bug-eyed spore erupting like new land from the mouth of a volcano. The old commons covered by water—a vile soup of rotten rats' eyes.

Testicle-eating worms. I disguise myself as a woman. A lesbian, possessed by another on my back, womb licked by a soft tongue. If you could suck on your own breasts, to which side of the lips would the pleasure reside. I would sit on so many faces. Frustration mutates. These are a man's thoughts. I am a man contemplating the certitude of death, considering new ways of life. Vicissitudes materialize on the horizon. A dreamer dreaming of an interpreter of dreams. I concoct heinous potions to suppress it. I'm sick today.

I'm at work. It's the middle of the night and I'm still at work. A man in a suit hunkers over a computer. Albert Einstein waves a white flag. Screaming, I run into the woods. I maintain wild aspirations. I walk through the trees carrying a book of poetry but fall into a pit—I sabotage myself.

The mother with the dark, penetrating eyes leans one elbow on the bar and asks for Jack & Ginger. She has beautiful black hair. We know each other, but we don't. She wants a ride home. On my lap, we kiss in the driveway. Her daughter sleeps inside the house. The mother can't stop moving, wriggling, writhing. My hand slips into her jeans and wet lips part; she was wearing a shirt but isn't as I push the bra up and free a pair of breasts like perfectly blown bubbles—POP. I admire them in the subtle streetlight. Hot, wild, delicious. I kiss and suck in a frenzy. Her mouth tastes like beer and smoke. I cum inside my boxers.

Usually, I don't remember the plot of wet dreams. But this one was so vivid with color, sound, layers of smell and taste lingering on my tongue. Pornographic films forsake plot to mimic wet dreams. In the dream, both genitalia are your own, like rubbing your hands against the cold. How can you distinguish between the rubber and the rubbed?

Twice, I've had wet dreams on strangers' couches.

Kerouac transcribes reality in his *Book of Dreams*. Burroughs writes subcutaneous fiction in *My Education*. I don't often remember my dreams—conscious nor subconscious, conscientious nor unconscionable.

In class on Friday, we read stories by immigrants from the textbook and I asked the students to define the American Dream.

Arturo: To prosper.

Khahn: That's the Vulcan dream, stupid. Mr. Spock always says, "Live long and prosper."

Fiona: I want to get my share now. I wanna rock Gucci and drive a Benz. I want diamonds and gold chains and the best money money can buy.

From the Boston Tea Party on, it's been about money. These kids don't know The Beatles, don't know rocknroll. They'd find *Money can't buy me love* a quaint notion. Che Guevarra said people don't agitate for change as long as a few morsels are tossed from the feast. The morsels haven't trickled down to this part of the world.

James: Just to be normal.

Melody: Patriot.

Laurence: It means being safe.

Georgie: Yeah, and owning a house. With air conditioning. It's hot up in here.

Georgie lives in an apartment with his mama, his sister and her kid. My own mother says I should buy a house. She offered a down payment if I committed to 360 monthly installments and thirty years of my life.

Me: I don't want a house. I don't want a yard. A yard means yardwork.

I don't know how to address Melody's one-word answer. Emma Goldman said patriotism was a "superstition artificially created and maintained through a network of lies and falsehoods." Patriotism stands watch over wealth and builds fences. Most of these kids live in shitty apartments and need change.

Mr. Stone: The market is on the buyer's side.

Mrs. Chins: The time is always now.

Mrs. Kasunic: Invest in the future.

I can't wrap my head around concepts like Stability or Prosperity. They seem surreal. I don't have tenure; my job is precarious. Kerouac dreamed about driving through France, where Dalí painted the signposts.

The American Dream is wet.

Me: I don't want money.

Wesley: That's why you're a teacher.

The students laugh.

Me: Is it true? I get paid, plus three months summer vacation. I can go to a doctor and retire with a pension after thirty years. I have everything I need—food, shelter…love.

Jane: Isn't it that if you work hard, you'll make it?

Me: That's what they say, but the people who work the hardest make the least.

Laurence: My mom works two jobs.

Melody: My mom gets paid less than a man in her office.

Me: Fiona, isn't your family more important than money?

Julio: They say Socrates let his family starve.

Me: Julio, why would he do that? Laurence, isn't time more important than money?

Wesley: The bosses invented time.

Me: Isn't art more important than money?

I went too far. Lost them. Khahn stares out the window; Fiona talks to Georgie off topic; Melody smiles.

What does it mean to be an American artist? Bukowski wrote forty-five books about drinking himself to death. It took seventy-three years. Hemingway turned to the shotgun after shock treatment. Hart Crane leapt into the sea from the stern of an ocean liner with his best work floating in his head.

What does it mean for a thousand Chinamen to die laying rail ties for Rockefeller while Rockefeller lives to be ninety-seven? I think of police riots, strikebreakers, anarchist bombs. Emma Goldman in exile, the Japanese grocer in Manzanar. The backs and bones of slaves who built this country. The Triangle Shirtwaist fire. A sick romanticism drives us to famous graves.

Maybe the students are right. Embrace the normal and disappear. Do normal people suffer their thoughts? Is it possible to feel horny just in the very tip-head of the penis? The call to stick cock in cunt is the call of the wild. My blood boils at Fahrenheit 451. My blue balls shrivel like the grapes of wrath. Appropriateness, social constraints, rectitude. What part of me (teacher, father, husband) can express desire?

I clutch my Art Spirit to rationalize my lascivious thoughts. Nudes pose for me. I jerk off, I lose interest. I get angry with myself. Run after truth and beauty. I yell at myself for sticking to safety.

We rock and roll through life and make the same mistakes our parents made. I'm a mole rat again, burrowing through the feces of my fellows. A waste of precious space, of air, of resources. I can do nothing useful for those who love me. I spit and it sizzles. Everything evaporates. I can't feel anything. My thoughts are rusty razors slicing innocent jugulars.

Out of the window of our apartment, a brown man clears debris from the vacant lot. He's worked all day with a scythe against weeds over his head. He bundles the weeds with coarse brown string and drags the bundles up a steep grade to the curb. A stack of student essays to grade sits on my desk next to a tall glass of iced tea. His skin burns under an unfriendly sun. I don't know how much money he earns, not enough. At the end, he'll see his success. A clear field spread before him where weeds once stood.

I wake on the cold compacted dirt. A pebble digs my shoulder blade under my sleep roll. I can't feel my numb face. My head aches. My mouth dried like a raisin in the sun. The sun. The sun rises over Stonewall Peak, which looms over the campground. The boys' sleeping bags are scattered through the clearing on a thick layer of pine needles. A squirrel scampers over a boulder and springs into a tree. His bushy gray tail provides balance. Mr. Stone tends the camp stove. He's wearing gloves, a plaid wool cap with earflaps and a thick jacket. His gray beard has grown thicker on his face. The early hour, the brisk air, the moments awake before the herd have invigorated him.

"Good morning."

The membrane of my sleeping bag protects me from the elements. Moist inside like a living tissue, a lung or uterus—I suspect nocturnal emissions.

The American dream is like fucking and being fucked at the same time.

Wesley Wilson

The last yellow school bus RUMBLES out of the campground on its way back to the city. Mr. Blythe drove up in his Suzuki Samurai and two of the parents brought vehicles in case we need to escape. I can wander off into the woods with my sleep roll, a pod, a life raft in a great green ocean of trees. The worker ants carry camp stoves and coolers full of hot dogs up the trail to the campsite. Kids run, jump, tag and frolic shaking the long bus ride from stiff limbs. I hear the word "faggot." Georgie struggles to manage his sleep roll. Vomit Boy hangs his head between his knees while a girl from Mrs. Tekhne's group pats his back sympathetically. She's young. Her hair, cut into a dapper black bob, hangs into her eyes above a face characterized by a demure seriousness. Her jumper seems much too stylish for roughing it in the mountains.

"Everybody line up."

Mr. Blythe shouts through cupped hands. I notice his designer hiking boots and Patagonia windbreaker.

"All right, line up."

Mrs. Tekhne flaps her arms and herds a group of children toward the staging area.

"Everybody line up."

The lines form slowly.

"Pass the word to our group to line up."

Instead of yelling, I whisper to Julio. He's a good kid. Knows how to draw. He tells Laurence who tells Georgie who tells Fiona.

She takes it upon herself to yell.

"Line yo sorry butts up."

Mr. Stone pulls out his big classroom voice.

"You have ten seconds to line up."

As the lines form, Stone, Kasunic and Blythe's lines are straight, but my scattershot line, like Mrs. Chins' line, spreads out in a disheveled mess.

"Hands up, mouths shut."

I put my hand up. The other teachers raise their arms. Children's hands go up, a contagious silence moves over the group. We've imposed classroom on the wild. Mr. Blythe and Mr. Stone count the children. Stone counts the limbs and divides by four, multiplies and extracts the square root. He's a math teacher. I recognize my twenty-four. Blythe counts again. He checks the roster.

"Who's missing?"

"Wesley and those guys went exploring."

TEENAGERS DEVOUR MOUNTAIN LION ON SCHOOL TRIP

Everybody in line sounds off, "Oooo." Mr. Stone and Mr. Blythe look angry. A crucial moment won't escape them. The other kids shout into the trees.

"We-s-s-s. We-s-s-s-l-e-e."

The calls remind me of my mom shouting, "Here kitty kitty" waving a tin of smelly cat food. Entropy eats at the sound waves dispersing the shouts to chaos.

Mr. Stone's voice cracks as thunder.

"We're going to wait here, in the sun, until they get back."

Everyone freezes. The light wind dies off, the trees fall still. How a voice can be so loud, no one knows. A veteran teacher, Stone has taught for thirty years. He knows all—does all. He swims laps at the community pool before school; delivers speeches at Toastmasters. He's been a scout master, an assistant baseball coach for his son's team. A community volunteer—he monitors the polls, organizes community clean-ups. Has two kids bound for college. Stone walks in the moment of the eclipse and steps outside of time.

Mr. Blythe jogs into the forest like he's having a Nam flash-back. He bounds over a fallen log and vanishes. We stand in the sun long enough to gain awareness of it. After a minute, I hear rustling and see a flash of brown on the hillside. A deer with full antlers.

My glance shoots from Georgie to Fiona to Vomit Boy.

"Wow."

"Look."

"What's that, Mr. J?"

"A deer, a buck."

My line stands like a crooked man in a crooked lane. All of my charges are present. I'm cool. We wait. The oppressive sun proves autumn the tail end of summer. Behind us, in the trees we hear a woodpecker's tap. The wind lifts a swirl of pine needles from the forest floor.

ROARRR.

A cacophony rises out of the trees, like a lion's roar mixed into the soundtrack of a tornado tearing the roofs off mobile homes in Arkansas. Two long minutes later, Mr. Blythe emerges from the woods with Wesley and the other boys. The boys are cowed, penitent, heads down. Blythe's muscles bulge, the swollen veins in his neck pump redness into his flesh. With his latissimus dorsi flared and biceps pumped, he resembles Lou Ferrigno.

Stone metes out the punishment.

"These boys kept their fellow students standing in the sun because they didn't follow directions."

Mustering the enmity of their peers is a dangerous game. He's hammering so hard, even I'm scared. The lecture goes on for minutes. Mrs. Chins exercises the right to remain silent. Her facial expression flush with contempt. Mrs. Kasunic and Mrs. Tekhne strike stern, grim and terrible postures, more like prison guards than schoolmarms. I'm thinking about the character who got beaten with bar soap in a pillowcase by the other recruits in *Full Metal Jacket* and the scene from Coteau where the prep-school boys, ordered by the headmaster to discipline themselves, hung one of their peers by the neck until he was dead.

"These boys will scrub the outhouses before we vacate this camp."

His raw red face has called on extra blood from the heart. The student mass remains quiet, guilty. I don't hear a peep of dissent, nor even a mocking, "Ha ha."

"The next person who wanders off gets a ride home in my truck."

The Suzuki's pastel blue glistens in the sun. I witnessed a conspiracy to catch the students in a melodrama of control. Almost everyone can see that Mr. Stone and Mr. Blythe are in charge. Everyone except Wesley.

He steps out of Mr. Blythe's shadow. A lanky contender wearing a branded tracksuit. He's on stage, into the spotlight, like in my class, ready to speak his mind like free speech exists, like he believed something I told him.

"I ain't cleaning no stanky bathroom."

One-hundred and forty-five kids roll out with belly-deep guffaws. HAA, HAA. The gray squirrel, antlered buck and spotted doe peer from the forest. I laugh and the world laughs with me, but Mr. Stone doesn't smile and neither does Mr. Blythe. Even Mrs. Chins stays uncharacteristically tight-lipped.

"Put your gear in the truck. You are going home."

He escorts Wesley to the truck. Mr. Blythe closes the passenger door. Wesley sits like a game show contestant in an isolation booth. The clock ticks. One recalls the traveling music from Jeopardy. Students and teachers witness a single tear slide down his cheek. He doesn't know the answer, the buzzer XXX sounds game-over.

"I'll return in three hours. And if I need to drive anyone else home tonight, I will."

The tires of the Samurai spin on some gravel in the parking lot as they decamp. True to his word, Mr. Blythe returns after three hours to find us cooking hotdogs on the Coleman stove. He got himself a vanilla latte and fast food from In-N-Out.

Downtime

"I should have pulled that stunt. Driven a kid home who climbed the wrong tree or littered. Arturo dropped an American cheese plastic wrapper on the trail. I picked it up myself. You boost credibility in the authority racket by chewing kids out. But no, I picked it up. Mr. Stone confiscated thirty flashlights. It never crossed my mind to commandeer a flashlight. I didn't yell at anyone. I played and got run ragged by questions, comments and plays for my attention. The kids want attention. Wesley got an hour and a half from Mr. Blythe. He expected a long private lecture on attitude adjustment, full of "time to grow up" and "maturity requires discipline," but poor Wesley didn't foresee an hour and a half of disappointed silence. Most of these kids are so used to negative attention—it's like ketchup slathered on a hot dog."

"Can you pass the potatoes?"

Alaska wears that orange dress I like; Caledonia passes the potatoes.

"Can you pass the corn, mama?"

"Sure baby."

Caledonia takes after her mom.

"We don't talk about important things in the classroom. We won't ask Wesley why he mouthed off or analyze how the inquisitors sacrificed him for control. At this level, it's difficult to sustain any conversation. The closest we get to a discussion about death or sex is the trade in 'shut ups' and 'fuck yous.'"

"Mommy, what's for dessert?"

"Do you remember when that little girl wrote in her journal how her dad slapped her across the face? Said she peed her pants. That was a rare glimpse at the real. The closest we came on this trip were corny campfire songs."

Caledonia stuffs a spoonful of food into her mouth.

"Slow down, Cali. You eat like we never feed you."

I poke at my food.

"Where has my dog Pinto been?"

"What?"

PPPPT.

"Dad, that's gross."

"Rich one."

"You're too negative."

"I'm the Life Magazine photographer. 'Cough for me Leper.' My camera's loaded with black and white film. There's a Pulitzer on the far side of your misery. I'm a bloodhound. I see in the dark. I worship suffering from Dostoevsky on down. I bring it home and bathe in it like the Countess Báthory. I sleep with it. But I am not negative."

"What's Daddy talking about?"

"Nothing important. He's been drinking too much coffee since he got home from camp."

She wants to tell me about her own troubles, lovely in the candlelight. How does she cut those Betty Page bangs so straight? *Giant Steps* by Coltrane plays on the radio.

"My boss's boss came to the store today… a white glove inspection. The Dandruff Queen said I need to 'smile more' and criticized the way I keep my uniform in order. I iron the stupid shirt every morning. It's not my fault that I work with coffee, which splatters. It's not my fault we don't own a washing machine."

"I know, sweetie. If I can teach these kids to read and question and think critically, I'll create a better world."

We all chew our food.

"What do I make but melancholy basket cases like myself? Shit."

"Daddy said 'shit' at the dinner table."

"I know, baby. Ignore him when he's like this."

Alaska looks at me with upcast eyes. I'm out of line, a fourteen-year-old in a crooked line on a camping trip. Still, her best blue-eyed gaze has nothing on Stone or Blythe.

Days later, I squander a few minutes organizing my thoughts, which run amok. It's so quiet. I've listened to all my CDs. The radio never plays songs I like. One channel can be tuned in on our tv, unless you count background microwave radiation. A cold caught in the mountains or in the closed quarters of the bus grips my throat. I lost my voice even though I didn't yell—instructing like Aristotle in the outdoor lecture hall. Repeating instructions, battered and abused. On my knees. At the end of a long, silent rope, a friend calls to invite me to a Halloween party.

It's Saturday night in the big city. The bars are full. There's plenty to do, with money to burn. The bonfire of the dollar. The coal-burning steam engine: work. I work to play and play to forget work. There's an airport downhill from my apartment. A plane arrives or departs every three minutes. Another plane lifts off the runway, destination unknown—hits the clouds—and is gone.

Normal Street

The first time she came to the house, I told Alaska that I was going with a friend to see a band. I go out to see bands all the time. Alaska had never been jealous and I didn't recognize it on her face. Framed by the door, Mandy wore a thin cotton dress with no visible panty lines. I understood right then, but Alaska made sure to iterate her feelings later that night. She was upset and hurt. Said I couldn't handle it if she went to a movie with a guy she met a week before. She talked to her friends about it and they all agreed. But I don't want to live under their morality. Even if I wanted to run off with a beautiful, intelligent woman, wouldn't repressing my desire make us both unhappy.

When Mandy invites me to a Halloween party, I'm split. Mr. J wants to nurse the ass-end of an illness and listen to old records, but my pirate nature grins like a swashbuckling band of rogues promised an equal share of the adventure. Assault on the Spanish Main, eh? Plunder, you say. It's the teacher's illness, which he picked up at school, the pirate reasons. Arrgghh, says the pirate.

"Mandy, let me call you back."

I hadn't bothered to put a light on. I slip Samhain's *Initium* onto the turntable. If Danzig's invocation of the season can't rouse me, nothing can.

This is the night to feast and dine. This is the night to laugh at death.

As the music builds to the part that sounds best turned all the way up, the phone RINGS again.

"Hello, son. How are you feeling?"

"Just a second, Pops."

"Hello? Hello?"

"Hi, I'm alright, I guess."

"Alaska said you missed work."

"Yeah. I feel a little better now. I'm thinking about going to a Halloween party in Hillcrest?"

"Isn't that the gay neighborhood?"

"It has that assignation."

"Why would you want to do that?"

"Mystery, doubt, uncertainty… and you know, like The Flintstones used to say, *we'll have a gay old time.*"

"You have responsibilities now. You're a teacher. You can't waste your time in the joints. You have a family."

Our conversation drifts like a cloud into the weather and since I don't follow sports, there's nothing more to say, so we hang up. Alaska took Cali to visit her parents and left me alone in the dark house with balled-up tissues on the floor, a pint of orange juice and a quilt wrapped around my shoulders. The phone RINGS again.

"Hey, Babe."

"Hey, honey. How are you feeling?"

"Better."

"What are you up to?"

"Thinking about going to the Halloween Street Party with Mandy Chiupin."

"Mandy?"

"Yeah."

There's a pause. I suck in some post-nasal drip and swallow it.

"Are you sure you're feeling okay? We need you to get healthy."

On Friday, I played hooky with my friend Loren Gitis, used a sick day, called for a sub and phoned in a lesson plan. Mary Chins O'Malley said the kids "tore The Sub a new one."

"I'll be alright."

"Dan, I'm serious. Caledonia and I need you."

"I'll be alright."

"Okay, honey. Have fun, but not too much."

"Okay."

"Bye."

"Love you."

"You too."

"Bye."

"Bye."

The sun rises on a gray, cold evening. Leaves jump back on trees. Flowers shake the wrinkles out of their mohair suits. The overripe fruit of summer dribbles on my chin. I'm alive. Life's hurrah before winter's icy grasp. Forget hibernation. The Day of the Dead reminds us to pay homage to our ancestors and Halloween screams live while you're alive and wake the dead.

"Hey, Mandy, I need a costume."

"Come on, Jimmy Jazz, a thousand fags in drag. Don't worry, we'll have a gay old time."

"Ha ha. I don't feel well, I'm sick. It'd be like trick or treating in a hospital."

"I wasn't allowed to trick or treat when I was a kid."

I'd forgotten about her deprived childhood, her parents were Calvinists or Zoroastrians. They banned the better rituals. She never had a birthday party.

"I don't know. I hoped for something more intimate. A few friends. Street fairs are too crowded."

"Come on, Jazz, I need someone to go with."

On the ride over, we don't say much. By the time I find a tape I like under the seat of her new wheels and fast-forward to a good song, we're on University searching for parking. She backs into an open space near The Center on Normal Street. I hear loud music.

"What a queer night?"

"Maybe you'll get lucky."

Mandy personifies sex. I can see why jealousy might infect Alaska. She wears a short skirt that wraps her thighs; black boots cover her calves. Mandy has licentious lips.

Revelers crowd Normal Street. Ten men in dresses sport bee-hives. A black leather stud with a zipper on his jock strap, pierced nipples and a biker's cap holds a horse crop in one hand and a leash in the other. His butt cheeks are smooth and un-blemished. He leads a man about my dad's age.

"I'm gonna whip her ass tonight."

Five waitresses, trays held high, circle around an old man in a suit.

"Thanks for nothing, Jesse Helms."

Mandy says, "Their customer."

"Ah."

A true poet catches things the less observant might miss. A hundred vampires in billowy tuxedo shirts glide past us.

"Blood, give us your blood."

A giant can of Cheez Whiz™ dances to the disco beat drubbing out of the PA. The MC, a dead-ringer for John Waters, heckles the contestants in a costume pageant.

"Number one through twenty move your tooshies to the stage."

A nun in a black habit walks up.

"Oh, my god!"

The MC lubricates his coif from a tube of KY and runs a comb through his hair. His razor thin mustache may be attached with spirit gum.

"This guy's the antithesis of funny."

"Jimmy Jazz, the crowd's on his side."

Her breath feels warm in my ear.

"Mandy, I feel like the only sober citizen at a Superbowl party."

"Jimmy Jazz. I feel alright. Look closely. Ev'ryone at this party came as their true selves. Just like you."

When two guys swim past linked together with a fish tank on their heads and faces made up like angelfish, I don't understand her meaning. A Boy Wonder in green tights follows a group of pregnant nuns who chug fake booze and puff unlit cigars.

"I laugh at your bad habits."

I hadn't seen anyone I knew until Helga Kropotkin pushed through the crowd toward us in a group with three or four MFA poets. The neighborhood laureate lives in an apartment not far from Normal Street, which takes its name from the city's first teacher college or Normal School. The Ed Center, where I interviewed for my first teaching job, stands on the site. She seems to be in good cheer, wearing a new thrift store dress and her trusty Doctor Marten boots. We haven't spoken since we drove across country together. Thirteen states in thirteen days. A road trip up through Nevada and Utah, across the Great Plains, through Minnesota and Wisconsin and down to Illinois. Thirteen days in a car will test any friendship.

Helga and Mandy hug and say something I can't hear off to the side. Helga pushes her flaxen hair out of her face and reaches to hug me too.

The poets wear .49¢ Lone Ranger masks—a simple masquerade. I attempt eye-contact with each in turn and they seem to acknowledge me, but it's difficult to tell what they think.

"Poets wear masks like bandits in liquor stores."

No response. The poets pan expeditiously left and right to catch every detail and run it through their respective poetry machines.

"If I'm here for eighty-one through a hundred, shoot me."

Helga laughs with or at me.

"You can't expect much; we're voyeurs here."

"I know what you mean. No one's hustled me or sold us drugs. No one's noticed us, we're invisible."

Orange cones and yellow caution tape mark where we can and can't stand. We're underneath a "No Loitering" sign near the intersection of University and Normal. A drove of police on horseback supervise the perimeter—ax handle truncheons at the ready.

"I don't see any drinks secreted in paper sacks."

"Come on, Jazz, look closer, everyone here got wasted before they left the house. Except for you, you're as sober as a semiotics lecture. Your sinuses look puffy, so if anyone sees you, they might think you're high."

A collective glitch in the equilibrium flows through the crowd. Telltale eyes beat inside furtive skulls.

A limo pulls behind the stage and a uniformed driver holds a sign that says, "Charger Girls." Eight cheerleaders wearing short blue and gold skirts with pompoms climb out. They pull at their skirts and adjust their fake boobs. Someone blows a whistle and they start their first routine.

"They practiced."

"Big ups from last year."

The cheerleaders turn, shuffle, clap, execute a high kick, and jump around.

"Kick them in nuts, pinch them on the butt, grab yourself a beer, listen to our cheer. We're here, we're queer, get used to it."

One of the poets bears her masque on a stick. I'm failing at being social.

"This sucks."

"Come on, they're funny."

"I hate football."

War-spent and ill—home and couch seem like worthy ambitions.

"I love this holiday. But somebody get me a fucking beer."

The MC looks tired. A guy dressed in military fatigues carries a dead baby. I'm sick, coughing. Mandy talks to one of the poets. Helga laughs with the crowd.

A guy covered in clear plastic holds a sign: Massengill™.

"Get this douchebag off the stage."

I watch the poets watch the revelers. Cheerleaders, nuns, the douchebag. They strike me as normal people, who work day-jobs, who want money and long to fit in with society. The douchebag probably drives a Mercedes SUV. Some of them are Republicans who vote to marginalize themselves. The voyeur poets in their dime store masks are the real freaks. They think in metaphor. Observe and dissect. Not one of them has had a real job. The difference between poet and poetaster is doggerel.

If I want to write, I should convert, make a joyful noise, dance, join the community, but I am not a joiner. I don't like disco or cheerleaders or nuns. Not even corrupt nuns. *I have no guilt; I seek pleasure; I seek the nerves under your skin.* Two groups in togas clash—a Greek crowns his champion with laurel; a Roman deepthroats a finger and pukes into a bucket.

"Was that real vomit?"

The whole poet gang arrived at once. June Farmer, a woman of about sixty, has brilliant silver hair. I hadn't seen her since she went north to care for her ex-husband. It's likely he passed away, but her natural orgone energy masks any grief. June huddles into Helga and whispers in her ear. Ethyl Piccolo, who opened the Green Door Book Shoppe in 61, came along. I always see them together, a foil to each other's complement. An article in the local paper said they joined the Hemlock Society—and stockpile secobarbital.

They're both friends with Mary Chins O'Malley and I half-expect to see my teaching partner in drag with a dildo stuffed in her pants under a beer gut and rubber plumber's crack. Since I missed school Friday, I wasn't privy to my colleagues' plans.

Professor Parsons lurks in the shadows behind June Farmer and Ethyl Piccolo. An inconspicuous observer, La Mujer Invisible. So, we have a full spectrum of poets: the naturalist, the formalist with her meter, the keen observer, the activist, the linguist, the historian, the rhymer and the narrator. I'm not sure how I fit in. The MC should come off stage and apply for the job of pun master general. Helga told me Professor Parsons has a special "Writing" hat, which she wears like a "Do Not Disturb" sign when she's working. I don't know what professors say to their students aside from prompts like "write from a different gender" or "describe your most shameful experience" or "trace your Diaspora." I wouldn't know what to say. "Go nuts. Live fast. Write what you know." Then again, "Stay home, take it easy and make shit up" sounds just as good.

June Farmer puts the ague of age in every word, phrases twist like wrinkled flesh, with unbridled exuberance. She conducted a poetry workshop at Ed Abbey Middle with some of my students.

"You seen Minnie?"

"No, Minnie's holed up with her jazz records."

"*Avant Pop?*"

"Yup. And *All the Things You Could Be By Now If Sigmund Freud's Wife Was Your Mother.*"

"Classic. How did my kids' poems turn out?"

She breaks away to shout at Tiny Tim.

"Tiny Tim wasn't gay."

"Tiptoe through the tulips…"

Tim croons and strums a ukulele.

"Great. Fantastic poetry. Mmm. Mmm. One student… Mary called him 'The genius who hadn't turned in a single assignment' wrote a magnificent poem. God. Fantastic. I'll publish his piece in the anthology."

"He almost didn't pass through the GATE."

The genius, ha. Mary Chins tried to nix Arturo from the poetry workshop, since the money came from the Gifted and Talented Education program. Divide and conquer, sift and sort, open the door but close the gate.

As she leans close, a hair from her chin pokes my ear. The music seems louder and so many bodies clog the street, it's difficult to move.

Carmen Miranda saunters past; June snaps a picture with her Instamatic camera.

"Bom bom, bom bom, bom, ba."

She sidles up to Miranda and shimmies her shoulders. June throws arms and snaps her fingers. And pretty soon they are in a booty shaking contest. June's ass moves in unexpected ways and it's clear Miranda can't keep up.

An hour rolls past and the costume parade seems so long the denizens of Normal Street must be changing costumes and getting back in the line, which stretches up-along across the down.

"Number sixty-nine."

The crowd cheers. A masquerader of non-binary gender in a Guns & Roses tee under a denim vest holds a cardboard sign up on stage: TRICK OR TWEEK. Queer sailors and proud soldiers hold hands. James Dean has his arm around one of the Togas. A dom-dyke drags her submissive on a choke chain.

Mandy buys eggrolls from a street vendor, but my taste buds are dulled, so I don't indulge. Two ragged men dressed as those bums who wash your car windshield at stoplights push through the crowd. They carry dirty rags and squeegees as props. One has a spray bottle filled with blue liquid. A Humboldt County Sheriff has a real gun.

"Hey, are you a real cop?"

The crowd shifts before she answers. Dusty Springfield struts by. The stage lights are like a house on fire. Mr. Burns and Smithers from *The Simpsons* stroll hand in hand. A crash of drag kings roll dice and crouch over their spats. A couple dressed as indigenous nomads stand in front of the stage and test the limits of verisimilitude. He bought a set of broken-hillbilly teeth from a gumball machine; her black fright wig looks dirty and matted with an expert sense of detail. The way they hold hands betrays a love gilded with generational poverty.

It's impossible to tell what is real. Elton John walks past. When a guy begs change posing as a deaf mute, his costume seems so ridiculous, overwrought, flamboyant and in bad taste, that he doesn't rake in a dime. Three Andy Warhols chat with Candy Darling.

Three young men, baring swimmer's torsos, tote a heavy Persian carpet. There could be a fourth man rolled-up inside, a dead blue arm hangs limp and bloody.

This guy named Rosa, who I knew from teacher school, emerges from the crowd dressed like Louise Brooks—flapper wig of jet black and sequin gown—Pandora's jack-in-the-box.

"You look ravishing."

"Mr. Johnson… What are you up to these days?"

"I work at a middle school."

"I saw you on Earth Day."

"We meet at street fairs."

The spectacle whirls, but I've lost my invisibility cloak. A forced march in the silly parade.

"Langston. James. See you guys later tonight."

"Lady Gay-diva."

A nude covered, mostly, by a floor-length blonde wig crosses the stage. She has a mustache like a cop.

"I'm working as a substitute, among other things. I just moved back to town."

"You can sub for me."

"I won't teach middle school. I hate the little homophobes."

He gives me his card: *Rosa de Luxe: masseuse, teacher, writer, tenor...* When we met in teacher school, he also wrote movie reviews for a local gay magazine. In Teacher Ed class he said he never met a textbook that wasn't "crap" and advised his fellow future teachers to write their own stories for the students to read. One of his creative endeavors presented a plan to curb overpopulation by sterilizing a whole generation.

"Oooo, look."

I catch the ass-end of a streaker blazing up stage left.

"Disqualified. He's not wearing a costume."

"Mr. Johnson, would you come to an after party?"

Mandy leans into Helga to say something. Rosa moves closer to catch my answer as the motley mob jeers in reaction to a police action near the porta-potties.

"James has an opium pipe."

"I'm with friends."

"I didn't see them."

Mandy and Helga are talking with Lulu Rivers and André Eel, the painter.

"Maybe next time, Rosa."

"Ciao."

"Ciao."

There's carnival music playing as a group dressed as a circus waits to mount the stage—a lion tamer, a clown, a ringmaster...

"Jimmy Jazz, André wants to join that group."

André must have a pint bottle stashed in the man bag slung across his shoulder—Mandy's wine personality emerges.

"He wants to show off his sword-swallowing act."

"June, as the bearded lady."

"Shut up, Jazz."

I knew Helga was still pissed at me.

"What should we do now?"

"How about trick or treating? Mandy never went as a kid."

"I went trick or treating. I wasn't allowed to go. Had to sneak out every year and hide my candy."

"Let's ask the circus if they want to go to my place and make a movie."

A glance shoots between the poets.

"Ethyl, as the tattooed woman."

"One tattoo. Tiamat, mother to gods. A single indiscretion."

"I can ride bareback."

"We need a contortionist."

"And clowns. We need clowns."

"Two-day party." June's arms are above her head again and the ass rolls like a temblor.

"Where's Dr. Parsons?"

"She must have slipped away."

I caught the climactic moment, out of the corner of my eye, before a long dénouement where Mandy and her friends debated who would ride with whom. It reminded me that we are amateurs among professionals. Ethyl, unseen by anyone else, popped a pill from a silver pillbox and washed it down with a long draught from the flask she keeps tucked in her handbag.

"Do you want a sacrifice? Do you want to laugh at death?"

"What'd you do this weekend, Mr. J?"

"Well… let's see Wesley. Uh… not much, getting over this head cold."

The Ark

My class doesn't know I'm a poet. They don't know much about my personal life. They don't know about the old sea trunk where I chuck the napkins and scraps of paper I write poems on: "Drunk Blues, Junky Johnny, An Atheist in New York, Eau De Cunt, Drag Queen #6… Too Sad & Tired to Masturbate, I write this poem…"

I taught twelfth grade AP English as a long-term sub once. The kids had read Ginsberg's "Howl" with their teacher. She exposed them to literary concepts like persona and they could separate character from author. But I didn't trust that they could separate madcap bohemian artist from teacher.

Last week, to my blunder and shame, I brought in a new anthology containing one of my poems.

"You didn't write no poems in that book, Mr. J."

I point to my pen name in the table of contents.

"Jimmy Jazz? Whoa. Check this out. 'Blowjob,' 'Condoms,' Whoa. 'My Country, My Cunt…'"

"That's enough."

I retract the book from his hand.

"I wanna read it."

A student tells a teacher he wants to read a book and the teacher says, "No." Curiouser and curiouser.

"You need to be older to read this."

I sound like Mr. Blythe.

"Wesley, the state grants eighteen-year-olds permission to smoke, buy lottery tickets, go to strip joints and read poetry. You'll have to wait."

He might find a poem called "Blowjob" funny. He might think Liz Belile made a convincing analogy in her sonnet.

…Fills the earth full of holes, feels like a hole in the earth.

He might giggle. The vocabulary words have been part of his prior knowledge for a long time. At first, whispered outside of knowing. Now, he says, "Suck my dick" once a day in the halls. Condoms. Blowjobs. The Principal should be grateful to see this boy grow comfortable enough with condoms to purchase one at CVS. When someone sucks his dick that first time—insatiable. He'll travel to India to study yoga with flexible ambition. Incidents with offal and accidents with the vacuum. In the poem, the poet wrote something like, "No way, would I suck your unwashed cock, you stink." How's he going to learn about cleanliness and consent and that a lover might give head but come swallowing time "prefer not to"?

"Okay, back to our study of the Mayan people."

"Do we have to?"

"Yes, Esperanza."

"The Maya were an advanced civilization."

"Yes, Julio. That's what it says in the first paragraph of the textbook. But how do you know?"

None of the students noticed that the Mayan myths in the textbook resemble the ones in the Old Testament of the Hebrews. I don't even know if these are real Mayan stories or propaganda manufactured by a textbook committee. In one of the Mayan creation myths, it floods after a rain of "40 days and 40 nights."

"What do the Maya value most?"

"Obedience," the class says in chorus.

"Yeah, but who wrote the story? Isn't it the case that the gods always profess the king's will? Today, we're going to compare and contrast the Mayan myth we read yesterday with the story of Noah's ark."

"We're not allowed to read the Bible in school. Ms. Woods said."

"Why do you think she said that, Georgie?"

"Because."

When I dusted off the black leather-bound bible my great-grandmother gave me to prepare for this unit, a note from her daughter, my grandmother, fell out. "I pray you will find Jesus in your heart."

Grandma watches tv, nurtures her fears and goes to church. In church, she hears about the sinful world her children brought into action. She sends pamphlets with titles like, "As Nasty as They Want to Be." She sent one about immigrants on welfare.

I found the story of Noah and read aloud to Alaska. The syntax seemed grievous for seventh graders.

"The kids won't understand the King's English."

I remembered how Rosa said to write stories for the students, so I gave it a shot.

Noah's Ark

There was once this guy named Noah. Noah was cool because he was righteous, meaning he had respect for other human beings. The angry god of the Hebrews was upset with people because they weren't acting right. So, God made a plan to scrap the whole mess and start over.

One day, right before the rainy season, God told Noah to build an ark, so Noah built it without asking too many dumb questions. If God says to build an ark, just do it. God said the ark should be really big so Noah could bring two of every kind of animal inside. Man, beast and bird. Noah, of course, wondered how he was going to fit all the animals in the world on a boat. He wasn't stupid.

Noah also wondered how he was supposed to coax all these animals onto the boat and what would keep the lions from eating everyone. In the end the animal question wasn't a problem. God let the animals know a big flood was coming and they were so happy to live that they overcame their natural instincts. Even the lions agreed not to make trouble.

When the animals showed up at the boat, the townspeople were curious. "What's that tall pink dodo bird?" Noah considered telling them he was starting his own circus, but he wasn't much of a liar. God chose him for the job because he was righteous, after all. So, he said, "There's going to be a big flood and you all are gonna die." No one believed him.

When the rain started coming down, it did not stop. It rained for forty days and forty nights. The floodwaters rose and washed most of the townspeople out of their beds. That's what they get for being so lazy and nasty. The townspeople scratched and clawed at the side of the boat. Noah couldn't bear to watch, so he went below deck into his cabin. The monkeys and hyenas laughed, which didn't make the drowning people feel so good as they died.

After forty days of floods, every single living creature, not on the ark, was dead. Except fish and the sea-faring mammals (who were innocent of sodomy and other perversions). After a few weeks, the water receded and God told Noah to be fruitful and multiply on the new earth. Noah was worried that his children would blow it like people did before. God read his thoughts and assured Noah that he would never destroy the earth with a flood again. And to protect Noah, he gave him a few laws to live by:

1. Be prepared.

2. Respect the rights of others.

3. Be kind to others.

4. Respect property.

5. Behave safely.

"It's a tad blasphemous."

"As my friend Cecil once said, "Blasphemy is a victimless crime." Did you like the story?"

"I liked it. Except for the sodomy part."

"The town was called Sodom, no?"

"I gotta get it past the woman in the copy room at school. She wouldn't let me reproduce a section from *Catcher in the Rye* because it had the word 'crap' in it. 'Who are we to edit Salinger?'

She wouldn't print it and I had no backup plan, so I blotted the offending word with Wite-Out and stamped CENSORED. The next day, she asked the school librarian to remove the book from the shelves."

"I'll give you guys five minutes to read the story silently, Juan sit down, and answer the questions on the board."

Twenty-five sets of eyes scan the handout. Juan sits but stares into space until, bored, he throws a pencil eraser at Oscar. Fiona finishes the story first. She has a paper out and squints at the board—expresses no personal reaction. At the five-minute mark, I hear notebooks shuffle and whispers.

Next period, I change tactics.

"Okay class, look at the story in front of you."

"What story?"

Arturo waves Laurence's paper in his face. Laurence grabs for it, the corner tears.

"Excuse me, let's be kind to others."

"Korrey, can you begin reading the story aloud?"

"Do I have to?"

There's a pause. He reads the first paragraph in a broken, stuttering voice. The students take turns reading. Laurence pronounces sodomy, "soda-my."

"What do you think?"

A group of girls share photographs behind a notebook and stash them away as I move closer.

"Both stories had a flood."

"Good observation, Melody. Why is that important?"

Silence. The clock shows five minutes to kill.

"God made the school rules."

"No, stupid. Mr. Johnson wrote that."

"Thanks, Laurence and… Korrey. Anything else?"

Silence. Three minutes remain on the clock. The students close their notebooks and shove them into backpacks. Roger, in the back of the room, has fashioned a peashooter from the hollow of his ink pen and shoots a wet wad at Laurence but hits Arturo's desk. I put my hand on Arturo's shoulder and ease him to his seat. My Doc Martens squeak on the floor. Roger puts the pen and several tiny pieces of wet ammunition in my extended palm.

Melody raises her hand.

"Yes, Melody."

"God gave Noah the rainbow sign, no more water, the fire next time."

Dirty Little Book of the Toilet

My neck CLICKS as I turn my head to look at her. It's happened before. Sometimes it "goes out" altogether—a pinched nerve. It's not magic, not some cosmic sign augured like an omen. Stress related, I read. The twinge correlates with trouble down the road, like an old man's knee predicts rain, maybe because trouble always waits down the road.

"All right, everybody sit. I know we don't usually do anything in homeroom, but I'm under pressure to 'Use Time Wisely.'"

"That's not one of the five rules at Ed Abbey, Mr. J. They had that rule at my last school."

The rules posted on the bulletin board back the young man's protest, though some would argue it under #1) "Be Prepared."

Fiona talks to Stephanie, the white chola, and Khahn walks in late. He slides into a desk.

"I want to know you guys better."

Korrey flosses his teeth; Laurence has his head on the desk. The statement garners no reaction; the kids look bored, sleepy. Georgie pours a half-pint carton of milk into a small cereal box. Chocolate-Frosted Sugar Bombs.

"Let's form a talk circle."

The room falls silent. Khahn walks out the door.

"Hey, Laurence, wake up. Pull the door shut for me. I want a closed-door session."

Ask them to talk, and they clam up. I'll remember that next time I need a moment of tranquility. My vocal cords aren't helping. The doctor said nodes dotted the cords and alluded to surgery. Alaska thinks I lose my voice on purpose to avoid communicating. Like the other day when I burned my hand on a cup of herbal tea I pulled from the microwave and screamed in pain, she said, "I told you to watch out for that cup. You don't listen to me."

"You can't talk about anything at school. Taboos everywhere. You know, inappropriateness. Or the kids aren't ready to listen. No res-"

"Excuse me, pass the salt, Caledonia. Dan, I'm surprised you want them to talk about important things at school when you never talk about anything important here."

"I talk."

"You talk about that fungal growth… and bodily functions. 'Honey, check out this dump I took. It's fascinating. I see the image of The Madonna in this pile of barf.'"

"Alaska, honey, this bizarre growth on my hand could be a tumor or a bite from a Cuyamaca Wolf Spider. It's not dissimilar to a sea anemone. Look."

I offer my hand for inspection to the class.

"And I did see the virgin mother of god in a pile of vomit. Derelicts have been canonized for lesser miracles."

"What's a see nemoney?"

Loquesha lives seventeen miles from the tide pools at Sunset Cliffs but has never been to the beach. When I was her age, a man pulled an octopus loose from the rocks. It curled around his fist and the image, evidently, curled around my mind.

I haven't written much since I became a teacher, except about Noah. I was sitting on the toilet the other day, thinking, when I got inspired. Before it came out, I didn't know if it was a poem or a short story. In the end, I wrote a pamphlet like the ones my grandma sends in the mail. I called it *The Dirty Little Book of the Toilet*. On one level, it described bowel movements. I scribbled observations like "makings of log cabin in Kentucky wood" and "four still sea lions in a yellow tide pool lagoon."

Alaska looked at it like I'd gone mad.

"Monitoring body functions contributes to a healthy lifestyle. I'm going to assign *The Dirty Little Book* to my homeroom as a writing prompt."

"Do you want pictures, Mr. J? Or just words?"

"Just words? Hmmm. If you can draw, draw; if you can sing, put it to a beat, but I want the words too. I want to see the picture in the words. This is a writing assignment. Everybody who shits can write."

From this point, I discuss the most intimate details of my life with the class. Whatever Alaska and I discuss lying in bed at night, I share with my homeroom the next morning.

"Dan, why don't we discuss our problems?"

Alaska impels a momentary aphasia with "Dan," rather than Jimmy or Mr. J—there are family names and dubbings, christened and guru given, but the best names, found on the streets, fit like worn in shoes. My immediate family still calls me Dan or Daddy; my mother calls me Danny. My great-grandmother used to sing my name, "Oh, Danny Boy."

"I don't feel like arguing."

"I didn't say argue; I said discuss. If we don't discuss, we argue."

My neck hurts.

"Apparently, only I see the humor in arguing about whether we're arguing."

"I think it's pretty funny."

Georgie slurps a spoonful of cereal.

"You should listen to her, Mr. J. She said 'discuss.' If you can't tell the difference, come to my house."

Alaska continues talking, but I've mentally left the scene. Sometimes I become part of the night, roll over the sky like a cloud, the ceiling for all things. Each city light a hearth burning electric kilowatts. I'm a dead man. I'm a teacher. A dead man. A teacher. I'd like to leave the house. As a boy, whenever I was ill , my mom was so kind—she would put a cool rag on my head. Since I became a teacher, I've been sick. A scrawny immune system bullied by lifestyle.

"I wish that I was dead."

The droll statement explodes like a train wreck and throws Alaska from her seat. Debris and twisted metal fly. A steel bar crushes and cripples her spine. There's a pause while I look up from my sickness.

"Can I go to the bathroom?"

"Why won't you talk to me?"

She's screaming now, but I'm inside my sick self.

"You wanna be dead? I wish that you were dead. I was awake last night worried about you, wondering where you were and I caught myself thinking, if he wrecks the car, I can find someone who cares about me, who won't ignore our problems, who thinks I'm important."

"Where were you, Mr. J?"

Alaska has her head buried in the pillow. It's after noon on Sunday, but she hasn't bothered to dress. Caledonia plays in the other room by herself. She's built an imaginary world with an invisible playmate. I ask her what sort of game she's playing with a little blue piece of string. "I'm not playing, I'm inventing with it."

"Alaska, I need to get some work done. Can we talk about this later?"

I massage my own forehead. I'd like to pull the skin up like a Tupperware lid and release some of the bad gas in my brain.

"No. It's always later, when is later? Now is later. You fucking asshole."

She wouldn't call me "asshole" unless she were really mad. I'm not here. I can't hear. I'm inside a bottle.

"Later, you'll be writing; later, you'll be grading papers; later, you'll be hanging out with your friends. Later, you'll be drunk or be sick from being drunk. Later, you'll be hanging from a fucking rope in the shower…"

"She said that?"

"Whoa."

"She pissed."

Sometimes writers stop writing. Rimbaud waves goodbye to Verlaine to run guns in Africa, Hemingway drives an ambulance in Spain. Celine, Pound and Hamsun sympathize with fascists. Bukowski works in a post office. The lucky ones pick up inspiration and start again. With amazing luck, you sit before the typer and hammer out a masterpiece. Maybe you can sell it and feed the family. If not, it all turns to shit, a waste of ink and paper. You can't justify those dead hours pecking at the keyboard as you discover the little girl can't read, a mess has fallen over the house and the big girl has to bite down on loneliness and neglect again.

"I don't know how to read."

I hoped to soothe her with a big, fat manuscript, like in that film *Henry and June*, you know, but she doesn't care. She'd like me to write a bestseller and buy her a house on the beach. "I wanted Tom Clancy and you give me what, Dostoevsky? Stephen King, I want King!" I'm rising to the top of the slide. I don't know what that argument was about, even though every argument in the last year has been, essentially, the same. Writers and teachers are supposed to have answers.

"No. No. Later, you'll be reading some goddamn book or going to a poetry reading or you'll be drinking coffee with Lulu."

"Who's Lulu, Mr. J?"

Lulu picked me up yesterday when I was supposed to fix the car. I don't think it's the battery or the alternator. Alaska and Caledonia went shopping with Helen. They took Cali to story time at the Bookstar in Point Loma, which we use as a library. We appreciate the comfortable chairs and wide variety of children's books.

Lulu and I grabbed espresso at Ground Zero near the MCRD and went to the record store across from the Sport's Arena to shoplift.

"Come on, Jimmy Jazz, it's easy."

Lulu's a film student. I've been in two of her movies. In the first one, I kissed a boy. In *Garden of Loons* I got naked and made love to a mannikin.

"I can't shoplift; I'm a public-school teacher. If I got caught…"

"Well, last week I had to sell all my CDs to these bastards to buy food, so I'm going to grab some music. You can't live without music."

She's right. Music should be free. So should rent and food. We go into the store. There's a long line at the checkout counter.

"Some of these shoppers are employees, loss prevention."

We're in the jazz section and she's scanning the alphabet.

"C-Coltrane, D-Davis, E-Ellington, F-Fitzgerald, G-Gillespie, H-Hawkins, K-Kenton… M-Mingus with Langston Hughes."

"W, X, Y, Z-Zorn. I need some new John Zorn CD's, somebody stole mine."

She pauses to scout the store.

"Act cool, see that hipster in the hip-hop section?"

"Yeah."

"Does he look like a hip-hop fan? He works here. He's pretending to browse."

She stuffs four Zorn CDs into her pants. His tight black T-shirt with the Rocket from the Crypt logo has a pack of cigarettes rolled in the left sleeve. A single cigarette has been lodged behind his left ear too.

"He's got a big cock."

I don't ask how she knows this. The jewel cases fit against the soft brown pubic hairs under her belt. Her coat covers the bulge.

"How do you know the sensors won't go off?"

"They put sensors on rap and alternative CD's, kid stuff."

I catch a few students scribbling notes. Alaska doesn't want to hear it. She clambers out of her warm bed and I hear the bathroom door shut.

"Sup, Lulu."

It's the kid with the big cock.

"Sup, Jeff. How's it going?"

"Pretty cool. Pretty cool."

He sniffles, wipes his nose with his hand. Lulu doesn't introduce me. The guy wears slick sideburns and a goatee. A chain wallet dangles from his studded belt.

"Doesn't he play in a band?"

"Everybody here does."

As we pass the sensor gate, I expect the alarm, but we're out in the parking lot. Jeff doesn't tackle me.

"I'm going to call Alaska. See if I should rent a video."

Lulu removes the discs from her belt and sets them in the car.

"Bullshit, you didn't call."

"I called. It was on the machine when I got home. We watched *Coffy* and *Female Trouble.*"

"Okay, Mr. Jazz, I'm going to grab some tacos."

Lulu crosses the street. Three jarheads stare at her incredible tits and heart-shaped ass. She blows a kiss over her shoulder and one of the marines follows her into Rigoberta's. Lulu claims she never pays for her own food.

I drop a quarter into the pay phone and punch in my home number—238-USEU. It RINGS and the answering machine comes on, "Jimmy, Alaska and Caledonia ain't here," followed by a riff from Social Distortion and a loud BEEP.

"Hey, Alaska. I couldn't fix the car so I went to grade papers and drink coffee with Lulu. I'll rent a video for tonight."

The school bell RINGS.

"What happened after that?"

"Tomorrow kids."

I sound like a frog. My throat has a stranglehold on me. I've got five minutes to steep green tea with honey.

"I also left a note saying I was going to coffee with Lulu. You want to rehash this?"

"Lulu wants you."

"We're just friends."

Lulu is a liberated woman who says what she wants and fucks who she wants, which Alaska thinks appeals to my bohemian sensibility. I won't say she's not attractive, only that she's not attracted to me.

"I don't want you to hang around with her."

"You can't tell me who my friends are."

"I've never told you who you could hang around with. I've tolerated more from you than any girlfriend would, I'm asking you to do one thing for me. For me. You're so fucking selfish. You never stick up for me."

The argument proceeds along this fault line. When she brings up the incident with Cecil at Pac Shores, I'm transported through time, thinking, swimming, staggering back to the night we stumbled along Newport Avenue in Ocean Beach. We walked past the head shop where Cecil bought that dick-shaped bong. The smell of dead kelp hung in the humid air and a small group of crack-hippies with dirty feet strummed mandolins on the sidewalk for change.

"You wanna buy a hemp bracelet, bro?"

"No thanks, bro."

"Where'd we park?"

It seemed like a good night winding to a close. Pac Shores still serves a stiff drink pretty cheap. The giant art deco clamshell removes one from the decade where your family competes with your day job for attention. Alaska put her arms around Cecil, but as she pressed against his chest, he pushed back. He threw his eyebrow up like John Belushi to say without saying, "I'm not a hugger."

"Were you molested as a child?"

"I could say what's been said before… but I won't."

This was the point where I should have interceded, told him off or punched him out. His reference to SF McBean's juvenile insult, "I wouldn't fuck her with your dick."

I didn't protect her honor that time either. SF McBean busted a guy's nose for insulting a girl he was living with. They'd been drinking too, in Mexico, and his girl ended up paying the broke-nose dude's medical bills. Five grand.

"Are you gonna let him say that?"

"You and Cecil were bantering. Friendship is a true democracy where everyone is equal and there are no hierarchies. Fair's fair. Friends and equals under the law. If I butt in, then 'girlfriend' becomes a special class above 'friend.' Isn't it better to hang out as equals? Besides, what he said was no worse than what you…"

This gone look came into her eye—a hand shot out and caught the pocket of my favorite blue Hawaiian shirt.

R-R-R-I-I-I-I-PPPP.

And then she was standing on Newport Avenue holding a square patch of blue and white cloth.

"My favorite shirt."

I should have laughed it off but I was pissed and scared. I don't buy clothes. I don't go shopping. She tore a perfect square hole, so that the nipple end of my tit stood erect in the damp sea air. I couldn't believe it. The car trip home was gutted by silence, absolute graveyard death quiet— which was good because I had to concentrate on driving. I was angry and still drunk when we got home and decided to sleep in my car. I rummaged through the apartment for anything of value, grabbed my Macintosh Classic, worried—sounds crazy now—but worried that Alaska might toss the computer out the window, like her cousin's husband who caught his wife flirting with some dude in a Kabbalah chat room online—I stormed out the door.

The school bell RINGS. My homeroom filters out as the first period class comes in. My lesson plan for today involves the students adapting Jim Carroll's *Forced Entries* into a dialogue.

> Jenny Ann: Roger's becoming obsessed with that weird museum you took him to.
>
> Jim: The Cancer Hall of Fame?
>
> Jenny Ann: Yes. Things in jars give me the creeps.

The next day at school, I hope one of my homeroom homies will share deep, real and intimate details of his or her own life. I'm surprised when they want me to resume my tale.

"How come your woman don't like Lulu?"

"Okay okay. Don't tell her this, like everything else in Room 13, it stays in this classroom. Got it?"

"We got it."

"Spit Family."

"Spit Family."

I've trained them to respond in chorus. Laurence said we should call our secret society "Room 13." So obvious, it's genius. I put the stone bowl in the center of the circle and they spit, by turns, filling it with saliva. This is the first ritual. We spit and keep spitting until each has spit. I drop a match on it and the butane I seasoned the bowl with before class blossoms into an impressive fireball.

OOOO, the girls call in response to the leaping flame.

AHHH, the boys respond in unison.

OOOO, the girls repeat.

Ahhh, the boys respond.

"All right. End of summer. Alaska got fed up with me and took Caledonia to live with her parents. We either broke up or were on a break. It wasn't clear. She meditated, did yoga and reinvented herself (adjusted her attitude, realigned her focus, redefined priorities). She called this "taking inventory." That was when she cut her Veronica Lake wave to the Betty Page bangs. She felt like I didn't care about her because I didn't want to get married. I was spending the weekend with Caledonia. I was trying to teach her to say "yogurt" but she kept saying "yo-gret." I would repeat 'yogurt' and she would say 'yo-gret." It was very frustrating. Finally, I asked her why she was saying "yo-gret" and she said, "Because I'm original." So, Alaska stayed at our apartment and I planned to stay at my mom's house. For some reason, I came back to the city to visit my dad. When Alaska called my mom's house to say goodnight to Cali, she found out I'd changed the plan. She called my dad at midnight and he told her I wasn't there, so Alaska started calling my friends. When she couldn't find me, she went to Lulu's studio on Spruce across from 7-11 and chanced a knock. Lulu opened the door holding a bottle of wine. When Alaska drinks, her intuition morphs into suspicion. When Lulu drinks, she likes to kiss girls. Lulu brushed against her breast reaching for the wine…"

Everyone seems to be listening.

"Lulu gave Alaska the phone number of a girl she thought I was interested in. Alaska called and hung up when the answering machine came on. Somewhere into the second bottle of wine, she started leaving messages like, "Stay away from my boyfriend, I fucked him last week, he's mine." The living loam soap opera plots are made from. But I wasn't fooling around with that chick since she had a secret boyfriend who was in my favorite band. Tension rolls like waves in a pool. Lulu got mad about being used in the fiasco (despite instigating it) and Alaska got mad because she thought Lulu wanted me for herself, but Lulu wanted the guy in the rock band. Are you following? The girl who liked the guy in the rock band wanted to marry him, but had to return to the small town in Nebraska she'd run from at age fifteen. Her father had been hospitalized for liver failure though they'd discovered he had a second liver, the remnant of a congenital twin, which had allowed him to develop a bar trick and some measure of local fame dazzling barflies with tremendous feats of drinking… Oh, and when I drove by our apartment at 3am, Alaska was making out with this swing dance teacher who dated her best friend… the chick who married the forty-year-old FBI agent. Got it?"

Classroom Management from a Barstool

I am the worst fucking teacher in the world. When I speak, a variable-message sign, like those ones on buses, flows across my brow: ACT STUPID. WHISPER TO YOUR PARTNER. SHARPEN YOUR PENCIL. I'LL WAIT. INSULT EACH OTHER. THROW PAPER.

As soon as I stop talking, the room coasts into silence. It's a technique they pushed in teacher school, but its engine is a weird combination of guilt and conformity. Hear me whine—I want respect and will use guilt to get it. Curse the soothsayer who calls this your future. I had this stupid conception that one earned respect. That respect was the authentic product of honesty and integrity. That education was the reward in itself.

"What kind of soap do you use?"

"Usually, Fiona, I just fling some sand on myself down by the riverside and shake off."

"No wonder you smell like that."

"Hey everybody, Mr. J is wearing two different socks."

I don't look down so he can't say 'made you look'—though I have no doubt Wesley is right. Open eyelids before the sun rises and dressed in morning darkness, one black, one navy. Sometimes I discover my socks twisted inside-out. My whole life has been inside-out and upside-down since I became a teacher. Matched or unmatched, Wesley comments on the socks and even when it isn't funny or misses the mark or doesn't make any sense, the group laughs. In teacher school, the education professors advised us to build rapport.

Is this what they meant? The inside joke and running gag bond groups like cement. I could turn things around, turn over all the tables and turn a new leaf, if only I had a pair of socks that said FUCK YOU. A special FUCK YOU just for Wesley. (Any bold-font FUCK YOU embroidered on the material would only join an incidental coffee stain on my shirt or rogue nose hair to incite more riotous whoopee.) The socks would have to say, "What are you looking at? With a name like Wesley Wilson, you're doomed to be the funny guy. You'll spend the rest of your life trying to make teenagers laugh."

I'm sitting in the bar, the bar of bars, my bar, the place where I like to drink because the jukebox understands my mood. The generation bar, the one we own for us.

I'm sitting in the bar after the first big teacher rally, before the strike, coming down off singing, *We shall not be moved*. I'm high from singing and sharing a pint with four other teachers.

"Hey, Suzy."

"Hey, Jazz."

I went to high school with the bartender. I remember how she helped the class cheat on tests in Driver Ed 1982. Someone would sneeze and she would say, "Bless you" for A , "Gesundheit" for B, "Salud" for C and nothing at all for None of the Above, which explains the ubiquity of terrible drivers on the roads. My students were born in 1982. She was a preppy with a pink cable-knit sweater knotted over her shoulders, but has since shaved her head and gotten some tattoos. She fixes cars now and rides a motorcycle. She draws that precious pint of the black and pumps quarters into the jukebox. Sculpting a shamrock in the foamy head of the pint with the artistic hand of a Brâncuși or Noguchi. The jukebox plays Hank Williams, Billie Holiday, Joy Division and The Germs. Aside from the teachers on barstools to my right, the joint is empty. The pinball machine waits in a corner. A pool of placid light illuminates the pool table, like a full moon spreading its glow over a foggy moor. One of my colleagues has had too much, a lightweight. I stare past my pint glass and watch the reflection in the mirror behind the bar voice opinion after opinion with a hearty 'Fuck The World'. A drunken reprobate in contrast to my quiet nature. Kids in school used to say I was shy—a label I reject—preferring taciturn, reticent, reserved or even meek. A Jehovah Witness told me at my front door that "meek" means teachable. The teachable shall inherit the earth.

"Fuck that prick."

The guy in the mirror looks like Milo from Descendents—he wears thick black-rimmed glasses, ala Buddy Holly, and has trim cut hair. A vintage shirt, a half-size too small, in ochre, zips up the front and could have been worn by a Tijuana barber in the 60s. His native New Yorker accent seems affected to bludgeon his listeners.

"That guy is a spineless fucking prick."

The political discussion sort of ends there and one of the other teachers wonders how the strike will affect his students.

"BF Skinner taught pigeons to play ping pong using positive reinforcement, so I give my kids candy when they study."

"Fuck that. The other day, I told this kid 'You got a 49—an F—which means you're fucking stupider than a guy who didn't even show up, a guy who got a zero.' I never had no respect for the teacher who told me I was a genius. The only teacher I ever loved was the guy who told me I was a worthless piece of shit. He played it like his time could not possibly be wasted by my existence..."

Breaking wild horses. Reverse-psychology. Doublespeak. Bribes. A mother hiding spinach in a milkshake. What about inexhaustible patience? Would I be a better teacher if I could channel this guy's belligerence? Would Socrates slap a kid down? Would Tolstoy? Nietzsche said, polite always.

Skin Mag & Stink Bomb

My teacher brain processes one hard case at a time. With Rosendo gone, Juan, Oscar and Arturo made plays for my attention. Oscar hides in his back row desk, a necessary evil since his broad shoulders block the smaller kids' views of the board. He has a book pulled around his face like a .49¢ Lone Ranger mask. He seems to have mellowed since I caught him passing a dime bag of marijuana to his friend Rudy in seventh grade. He might smoke the herb these days instead of tossing it around like a Nerf football. I've got the class quiet. I don't hear any idle talk. They're supposed to read, but at this point, quiet suffices. Arturo holds *The Autobiography of Malcolm X* upside-down.

Juan Maldonado peeps around *The Giver* for someone to pull faces at. Last month, Joe, the Security Guard called me on my lunch break, "Sup, Mr. J, we got Juan here, I confiscated something you gotta see." I carried my peanut butter and vegan mayo sandwich to his office thinking knife, gun, pipe bomb… chemical warfare. I leaned against a gray filing cabinet and bit the stub of a carrot.

"What's up, Doc?"

Juan sat in a blue plastic chair in the tiny room they use for interrogation, slumped over like somebody told him the truth about his mother or like his best friend had moved away. He was making eye-contact with the carpet—which they told us in teacher school shows respect for those about to punish.

He has wrapped his gutless mother around one of his dirty fingernails. His hands are always dirty, due, in part, to the perpetual absence of soap in the boy's restroom. He seems too big to whine when he doesn't get his way, he's much taller than me, and already two heads over his mom, but I've seen him use the broken record technique on her, repeating "please, please, please" like James Brown in a cold sweat.

"Juan was trafficking in pornography, Mr. J. I caught him passing this around the lunch arbor."

He unfolds an issue of *Hustler*—an exposé featuring shaved-pubes, pink labia and ostentatiously fake boobs. The porno magazine is about ten years old and the cover shows actors who look like Prince and Sheila E.

"This is no way to learn about sexuality, Juan. Thanks officer, I'll escort Juan to class."

Joe, the Security Guard gave me the magazine.

"I'm disappointed in you, Juan."

Joe, the Security Guard shook his head. Not sure why I expect verisimilitude and authenticity from porn, but fake boobs don't turn me on, and because the model didn't really look like Prince. The walk to class was a long march. I locked the magazine in the desk drawer.

"When do I get my magazine?"

"When your mom comes to pick it up."

"That's not fair. I got rights."

If he'd paid attention in class, he might have tried a free speech argument.

"You can't keep those Johnson. They're not mine. They're my uncle's."

His voice wasn't threatening or assertive enough to seem defiant.

"Sorry, Juan, but porn is not allowed at school."

"I'll take them home. Please, please, please."

"No, no, no. One more?"

"Please."

"No."

In teacher school, they taught us how to use the broken record too—one tool in a campaign of assertive discipline. Maybe Juan should become a teacher. He has asked me for the skin mags every day since and thinks he'll wear me down. Maybe that's how his dad met his mother. His mother has little control over him; she once gave permission to go to the movies about an hour after he was brought home by the police for boosting hip-hop CDs at the mall.

"How about if I bring my uncle?"

Is the jerk-off trade that thin? Is it supply and demand or are these particular numbers valuable collectibles?

Last year, a different kid had a magazine called *Famous Anus*. Mrs. Kasunic, the science teacher, confiscated it after a circuit around her class. She brought the skin mag and the boy to my room. She buttoned her lips together and shook her head like she'd never been more disappointed. A teachable moment for an anatomy lesson was in hand, but she let it pass. To the kid, she presented the steel-trap-jaw-face, but flashed an embarrassed pink smirk at me. Mrs. K was a doppelgänger for the cover model, though it was hard to picture the science teacher spreading her butt cheeks for the camera. I wrapped *Famous Anus* in shiny paper with a red bow and dropped it in the Principal's mailbox.

The year before, a kid named Marvin was caught with a nudie playing card he found in his grandfather's WWII footlocker. I was subbing for their usual instructor. His homeroom teacher made him do a report on pornography. Juan might benefit from such an assignment, though it could backfire with a 10,000-page Meese report slapped on my desk like an illustrated phone book. Writing an essay is better than copying "I will not jerk off in class" a hundred times, but using an assignment to punish seems counterproductive. Writing should be a sacred privilege. I've been on the Vice Squad three years, and Juan's pleas fall limp like the cum-warped pages of his dirty magazine.

Mr. Maldonado has decided to punish me for this violation of his rights by goofing around during silent reading. My voice aches from talking over student voices all week. I ask the class to be quiet, like they are now, but the serenity doesn't last. We hear Mr. Stone yell at some students from two doors down. "Sit, sit, sit." One of my students says, "He's talking to a dog." Yelling is like putting a Band-Aid on a decapitated head; it's not sustainable. My original plan was to model silent reading with the students. I haven't finished a paragraph of Bulosan's *America is in the Heart*. They force me to watch them every second. It's time to change activities and a few kids take journals out to record thoughts about the reading like I trained them. Others wait for me to tell them. The shuffle of notebooks pleases the ear.

Chaos breaks out in a slow, rolling wave from the back of the room. There's a skidding sound and tiny shatter of glass. Georgie, who I moved to isolation near the back, coughs. It's a stink bomb. I can't tell where it came from. No "Ha ha" funny prank—a toxic green cloud envelops the room.

"It stinks."

"It it it it it stink stink stink stinkstink stinks."

This is not my first stink bomb.

Fiona heads for the door.

"Everybody sit."

Fiona throws a hateful glance. My voice hurts, but I raise it anyway. The nodes on my vocal cords ache.

"We can't disturb the other classes' right to study. Everybody sit."

It's like a chapter from some book I had already written, a line of repetition from an epic poem. I block the door with my body and the smell seems to intensify.

"Let us out."

"Let us out, Mr. J."

On his knees, Georgie pukes whatever slop the free breakfast served this morning.

"Rapido Johnson. Let us out of here."

I'm thinking it's good that Vomit Boy is in math class when Fiona falls to the floor and pukes out her own breakfast. Events proceed too quickly to register schadenfreude or rethink the merits of authoritarian control. Is she sticking a finger on the back of her tongue? Hmmm. She's the first suspect for extradition to the World Court. With two puke piles on the floor, I'm forced to let them out. On the news, a terrorist released sarin gas in a Tokyo subway. They put a black mark in your employment file after mass-hospitalizations.

I have lost control.

"Georgie and Fiona go to the nurse."

The other teachers stick their heads out the doors of their respective classrooms.

"What are you guys doing out here? Please show respect for the rights of others to learn and study."

Mrs. Kasunic speaks to my class but seems mad at me. It's my job to head off disaster.

"All right, you heard it from the scientist; everyone back inside."

"No way."

"Get in there."

I must be making a monster face (like some evil naked mole rat) because they go in.

"It still stinks in here."

I use the emergency phone to call a clean-up crew and the Building Services Supervisor brings a mop and a shovel for the piles of vomit. He doesn't say anything while he mops the mess. Penitent, I flog myself with brambles. His silence makes me feel like I threw the stink bomb. The Building Services Supervisor controls the supply line for the entire school, so I might as well kiss those markers I ordered goodbye.

"Look."

Loquesha points to a stain on the floor.

The Building Services Supervisor picks up a piece of broken glass.

"Wake the armadillos. This vial contained hydrochloric acid—poison."

I pick up a stack of clean line paper from my desk. We should be reading Langston Hughes. I rip the sheaf in half, thinking I could tear a telephone directory and pass a slip to each student.

"If you know anything, write it on the paper."

Time is not on my side. The bell is going to ring to dismiss the class. The next one will need to come in. I will hear, "It smells

funky in here" all day. I shuffle through the ballots. One reads:
I think it was a stink bomb.

"Huh, nobody did it. We're going to sit quietly in this room after school until we solve this mystery."

"I need to catch the bus, my mom says I can't stay after school."

"Well, Wesley, my mom said don't let kids get away with throwing stink bombs in your class today, Honey."

My voice is gravel; I must sound pathetic.

"Maybe somebody threw it in from outside."

Julio adjusts his glasses by pushing them back on his nose.

"Notice how the direction of the splash stain points toward the door."

I want to believe my students respect me enough to play this game somewhere else. My mind fills with doubt, confusion and denial. We do another round of secret ballots but no one admits guilt. And no clues are offered. "I was reading," one note says. Georgie and Fiona return from the nurse. Fiona hands me a crumpled pass that smells like vomit.

"I'm not staying after school. I already got sick."

After school, Fiona sits in her regular seat. The rest of the class sits quietly. Mr. Stone and the other teachers post up around the room to help me interrogate the class.

"We're going to sit here until we find out who caused this. Acid can trigger allergic reactions. We could have a dead body on our hands."

I'm sitting in a chair at the front of the room. Everyone is guilty. They know who did it. They know who was showing off stink bombs in the locker room. The loyalty code of the schoolyard or the secret pleasure of watching their teachers lose control keeps them quiet.

"We will make them talk."

The questioning resumes with the usual suspects pulled aside. Mr. Blythe, Mrs. Chins and Mrs. Kasunic stand like pillars of marble. Stone looks into the mystery with expert eyes. My voice is gone. Laryngitis finished it off during sixth period. Mrs. Kasunic counts the ballots, counts the heads of the children. She sorts the data. No one is going anywhere. Friends and siblings gather at the windows outside. The classroom heats up like a crucible. We expect the truth to separate and float to the top. Even a lie could send us home. A martyr could save us. More secret ballots. One ballot offers a clue: *The flask came from the door, who was sitting by the door?*

Hmmm. Oscar occupied the closest desk to the door. Another ballot reads: *I think Oscar did it*. We put the heat lamp on but he doesn't crack. We do another round of ballots. This time one of the papers reads: *I did it, X. Oscar.* I heard several months later that Fiona gave him the stink bomb.

Arturo

On the second day of our camping trip, the kids relax and regress atavistically. A game of throwing-shoes-around develops. The chase winds in and around the trees near the camp while they wait for the breakfast hot dogs and warm cocoa. An entire pack of hot dogs went missing during the night and Mr. Stone is disappointed.

I'm sitting on a rock with Arturo. It's cold enough to see our breath. I've got my own black watch cap pulled over my ears and wear a red and black lumberjack shirt.

"Mr. J, why do you let these pinche kids take advantage of you?"

He's the toughest kid in school and has a habit of telling kids to "shut the fuck up" in my class. He wears his burglar beanie pulled low on his huge forehead. For some reason, Mr. Stone confiscated his Tone Loc sunglasses. His deep-set eyes dart around and see everything. He buttons his Pendleton all the way up tight at the neck like the vato locos in the park. He takes after his old man who took after the old man before him. Arturo's fourteen and has three dots (mi vida loca) tattooed on his hand between thumb and index finger. He has as many fights under his belt as a welterweight and likes to tell stories—about Juvenile Hall, about a robbery he pulled off when he was nine, about a drive-by shooting his cousin got caught up in. He talks about respect, about manhood, about survival. He would describe the conflicts as Man vs. Man, but they seem more like Man vs. Society. I particularly liked the yarn about his grandma running drunk through the orange fields of the San Fernando Valley. His other teachers don't seem to like him as much as I do. He can be rude, for sure, but their animus may owe a debt to their inability to break his spirit.

Mrs. Chins: "I wouldn't want him in my class."

Me: "Really, I like him. Rosendo was out of control, but Arturo's a natural poet and probably a genius."

Mrs. Chins: "Psshhh."

Me: "He reads upside-down for one thing."

He mesmerizes his audience. He's a performer. You can track the eyeballs glued to gestures as he reels the listeners in. He has spirit and timing. His punch lines leave us in stitches. But he doesn't read well, at least with the book right-side-up, and the short fuse on his temper explodes in broken noses. He swears in class. I'm not sure why he's been following me around the wilderness on this campout. He must prefer my company to the others who seem like children to him.

"I shouldn't need to control you, you should control yourselves."

He scoffs.

"Bundle your sleeping bags."

Mr. Stone yells through cupped hands from behind a wall of jack pines, so it sounds like a voice out of the woods.

I can hear Mrs. Chins cackle in front of the morning fire.

"Hee heee. Remember last year when I told Barbara Jackson, 'If you don't shut up, I'll kick your butt so hard, you'll be the seventh sister of the Pleiades.' Heee-hee-hee."

"Last year, we camped in the desert. We studied astronomy, stargazed. Barbara Jackson needed someone to kick her butt. She's a high school cheerleader now."

"I could get my cousin."

"That won't be necessary."

Melody combs her straight blonde hair. Her bedroll has been folded meticulously. Mrs. Kasunic counts her group and marks notes on a clipboard.

"Hey, Georgie, pass the word to Vomit Boy and the rest to clean our area."

Mr. Stone's voice rises out of the forest again.

"Pile your things over here; clean up this campground."

Wesley's accomplices are scrubbing the latrine floors.

Arturo follows me and yells across the compound.

"Yo, punk, don't mess with my stuff."

A scrawny seventh grader looks worried. He scampers over the hill, into the trees, like a leaf at the mercy of the wind.

"Like I was saying, Mr. J, my dad handed me a gun and said, Arturo, if anyone mess with you kill 'em."

I pick up my rolled sleeping bag.

"Where's your dad now, Arturo?"

"Folsom."

"Is that your fate?"

He's the dangerous genius society imprisons for its own protection. Mr. Stone's voice cuts in.

"Arturo, leave it like you found it. We're breaking camp."

The Strike

The world turns like a mimeograph printing dollar bills. Citizens turn in sync to grab a share. Grab with gusto, claws and balls out. Ovaries to the wheel. Our culture programs us to want. To want it, to want all. Somebody told me teachers were the antithesis of capitalism. Somebody told me public school teachers were the last idealists. Monetary respect for our "somebody's gotta do it" job traded for personal satisfaction: the world, after all, is bettered by our struggle.

Mrs. Chins hands me a button: I am a Priority.

"Some Bozo bigwig at the district office said, 'Giving teachers a raise is not a priority.' Hee heee. So, the union sent every teacher in the district this pin-back propaganda. This one is about respect."

She pins the button to her blouse.

I show up on the picket line with Hubert Selby's *Last Exit to Brooklyn*, suggesting a story hour. Maybe tomorrow I'll read the scene from Steinbeck's *In Dubious Battle* where Mac organizes the strike camp. I brought a picket sign, a box of sidewalk chalk, a boombox and a cassette tape—dubbed the night before—with solidarity songs.

It was early springtime when the strike was on…

I plan to pass the time humming civil rights-era spirituals and pogoing in front of the school to The Angelic Upstarts.

Let this strike, cruel strike carry on…

In Poland, they called it "Solidarnosc."

The teacher's union made "respect" the first buzzword, so I put Aretha Franklin's voice on the tape singing, *Sock it to me*. Aretha carries Ms. W through time to the fight for the ERA and she sings along, *"R-E-S-P-E-C-T."*

Music is the best painkiller and dancing is good medicine. So, I play Hazel Dickens' *Rebel Girl*, Joe Hill's *The Preacher and The Slave* and Paul Robeson's song about Joe Hill. My school year had been coming apart like my pants at the seams, so the strike offered a deserved, albeit unpaid, vacation. Inside the school, I'm on the faculty equivalent of academic probation. My team and the Principal handed down an ultimatum: *Improve classroom control or find a new job.*

The Principal isn't happy about the strike. He hasn't left the school site in days. For someone who talks like a dead Kennedy, he looks more and more like Nixon and seems to have borrowed Reagan's tactics against the air traffic controllers. His jowls shake when he gets in a groove. I picture him delivering sermons from the pulpit and stumping from a train—until his high blood pressure lights up his Tricky-Dick nose.

"The Edward P. Abbey Middle School is not like other schools. We are a charter school. That means our commitment to the parents and to the children remains paramount. We made a pact with this community. The charter trumps whatever nefarious business we have with the district. We are not bound by their limitations; we are not governed by their rules, and yet, as you are all painfully aware, we are scrutinized doubly."

During this meeting before the strike, he didn't use the phrase "Grant Money' nor mention the hoops those grants require us to jump through, but money motivated his speech as much as anything.

"Everybody is watching us. Lest I remind you of the stakes. Some people want us to fail. Being a charter school signifies that we will control the means, in a few years, to raise our own money through The Foundation, so this strike has no meaning for you."

Mrs. Chins was the only one brave enough to speak up.

"If the charter collapses or we transfer to a different school, we will be stuck with the same salary as every other teacher in the district. We have to strike."

She's the kind of person who would speak freely even if tenure didn't protect her job. Before she uttered it, I hadn't imagined a teacher resigning from this school voluntarily. It's the kind of ship you sink with.

Doctor Pullman stood squarely behind the Principal.

"We're going on strike like a bunch of truck drivers."

He isn't a real doctor and has no advanced degree. He writes the title on the board and students and visitors assume he's a doctor. Mrs. Chins jokes that he went to the County Administration building and legally changed his first name.

Doctor Pullman is inside the school teaching a class—a scab who crossed our picket line.

Billy Bragg sings.

Which side are you on, boys? Which side are you on?

My boom box pumps out the tunes. The music matches our mood. We march with signs and spirits high, loaded with vim, vigor and propaganda.

"Look at this guy."

Mr. Blythe leans on a picket sign like Paul Bunyan on his axe. A man wearing checkered suit pants, matching vest and a wide, striped tie approaches the school from the trolley station. He walks up the sidewalk on 61st Street like a robot and talks to himself. At the corner, he turns on a dime and swings a brief-case at his side.

"He's a sub."

"Hello, sir."

He responds with a series of binary BEEPS.

"Well, if that's who they've got to replace us, this strike shouldn't last."

On the eve of the strike, the union bosses set up a rally at Golden Hall downtown. Five thousand educators filled the bleachers from floor to rafter. Bob Dylan, The Stones and The Clash all played here. A man I didn't recognize stepped up to the microphone, touched it to see if it was on and sent feedback from the PA through the hall.

"PSST. Who's that guy?"

"The union president."

"The district says the coffers are empty. They offer us no new money. They are lying! They are lying! They are lying!"

Five thousand teachers ROAR and wave banners, signs and placards.

"You all know Chunky Sanchez."

Sanchez marched with Cesar Chavez and was in the fight for a people's park under the Coronado Bridge. He carries an acoustic guitar and raises a brown fist in the air.

"Power to the teachers."

HURRAH.

"It's about time I dusted this machine off, eh?"

HURRAH.

He struck a wavering, solitary E chord on the old guitar and began to sing an old slave hymn and protest song.

Like a tree planted by the wa-a-a-ter, we shall not be moved.

Soon, all five thousand of us had joined in. After that, a series of motivational speakers stoked the crowd.

"Our negotiating team is at the table, but those fat cats at the district office want to keep all the money for their own bloated bureaucracy."

At home later that night, filled with excitement, I lay next to Alaska in our bed with that tune reverberating in my thoughts.

The next morning, Mr. M, a computer teacher, strums his picket sign like a guitar.

"Check this out."

I mount my own sign like a wicked witch cackling on a broom.

"I'm Mrs. Chins, hee hee hee."

A sort of competition takes root and Mr. M digs the toe of one sneaker into a line on the sidewalk, bounces and tosses an imaginary ball to serve it with his picket sign cum tennis racket. I put two signs together and lift them as dumbbells. Together, we slip into our invisible canoe and paddle along the picket line.

"The union man said to keep moving."

"Lovely day on the lake."

One of the veteran teachers brought donuts. I start with plain cake and the first bite tastes too sweet. After that, I eat a strawberry frosted donut with multicolored sprinkles and because they are free, a third donut leaves me feeling sugar shocked. My teeth are coated and I need water. There's no bathroom on the line, but we can always run down to the Cotija.

There's a hectic window on the strike line before and after school when the kids come and go; the rest of the day is a blesséd monotony.

A parent honks support for the cause from behind the wheel of a GMC pickup while a guy in a dark blue SUV yells, "Get back to work. My kid needs an education."

Beginning teacher wages wouldn't invoke envy, but some veterans on the line earn fifty thousand dollars a year.

"Listen, buddy, I don't got medical bennies; quit your whining."

"Join a union. Ask if it would be 'the greatest country in the world' without the struggle for the eight-hour day or if children slaved in meatpacking plants."

On the third day, two carloads of wild teenagers speed past the strike line, honk and shout support. The driver of the lead car, a lowered Nissan, brakes to pull an illegal U-turn and the Ford Taurus behind him smacks into his bumper. A headlight falls to the street like an apple from a tree. I laugh out loud. TSK TSK sounds emanate from Mrs. Kasunic and Mr. Stone. Teens jump from both vehicles, assess the damage and run a circle around the cars. A boy shouts, "Sup, Mrs. G." A girl from the passenger side of the rear car picks up the headlight and jumps back in. Both cars speed off.

Mrs. Chins crossed the picket line at a ridiculous hour, before sunrise. She decided at the last minute to join the scabs inside. I feel betrayed. I don't know how we'll work together.

"I'm doing it for the kids."

"Didn't you say we had to strike for the kids?"

Some teachers say she needs the money. We hit the strikebreakers who cross in front of us with our hardest evil-eye teacher glares because Mr. Stone wouldn't let us bring bats.

On the fourth day, the union anticipates our malaise and stages an afternoon rally to boost our spirits. Chunky Sanchez plays the song again.

We shall not be moved…

The union reps rehash the fiery speeches and dismiss the teachers for a rare hour-long lunch. At school, I'm allotted thirty-five minutes to eat—if I'm not busting kids for porn or dope. I decide to spend my hour at home, where Alaska and I make beautiful love with the stereo playing PJ Harvey. I remember what it's like to be unemployed. I let the juice from her lips dry on mine and wear the invisible mustache to the strike line.

"What's this strike all about, Mr. J?"

Georgie, Vomit Boy and Julio came out to talk with us after school. Vomit Boy has the sniffles and wipes his nose with the sleeve of his jacket.

"The teachers don't feel respected."

"It's about money, isn't it, Mr. J?"

Georgie says this with a sullen voice. His family has been on welfare his entire life; he's tried to buy cigarettes with food stamps for his mom and gone back-to-school shopping at Goodwill.

"What's school like without us?"

"The substitute used foul language. I learned some new vocabulary."

"One teacher man bribed the sixth graders with nickels, so they'd do the worksheets. At least that's what Fiona told me and her cousin told her…"

"The sub in Mr. Stone's class showed a rated R movie."

"Strike school sounds more fun than regular school."

Every VCR in the school is in use. Forget math, forget science, forget writing and silent reading. The routines we worked hard to instill are breaking down.

"My daughter says that the Principal at the high school locked the kids in the gymnasium."

Mr. Stone pats Georgie on the back and smiles.

"The main piece of education going on in public school this week is about strike actions. I remember when my teachers went on strike in 6th grade. That was cool."

"It's our duty to strike every ten years. Show the kids the power of union organizing. If they don't learn it from us, the man wins."

It's funny to hear Mr. Stone talk about "the man" like he isn't the man. Flashing back to his hippie days in SDS at Berkeley.

On the fifth day, the strikers wait for the scabs to drive out after work. As a car pulls from the faculty parking lot, the chant rises.

"Join us. Join us. Join us."

In between chants, we speculate about the strikebreakers' motivations.

"It's about the money."

"They're in there like we're out here. For money."

"Yeah, money. But Ms. W, who has breast cancer, walks the line and even Mrs. Kasunic has a picket sign."

"The scabs will accept the raise and rights we suffered for."

Mr. Y spits in the gutter.

When Joe, the Security Guard comes out, the chant rises.

"Join us. Join us. Join us."

We jump up and down.

"You guys are the silliest strike mob."

Joe's not teaching, so he isn't technically a scab. He dresses more like a drug dealer than a security guard, in a leather motorcycle jacket. His hair is cropped at the top and long in the back. His acne scars age him. The teachers on the line gather around his car and delve for information.

"Bet you've got your hands full."

"What are they doing in there?"

"Tell us everything."

"The Principal held a meeting. We miss you guys."

As he drives off, I'm practicing my Johnny Carson golf swing with the picket sign. A scab driving a beige BMW comes out behind him and the chant resumes.

"Join us. Join us. Join us."

The teacher behind the wheel lowers her head in shame. She started teaching at Ed Abbey a month ago, so no one really knows her. The next car doesn't stop at the driveway and scatters the teachers. The driver peels out into oncoming traffic and nearly sideswipes a Buick. The scab crouches in the back seat, covering his or her face with a coat.

"Who was that?"

"Don't know. I'll bring my video camera and tape them as they drive out."

The next day, the media reports on who's teaching the city's children while we're on the line. When a seventeen-year-old senior shows up at the office in a suit and tie at his own school and is given charge of a classroom, we smell victory, but the district and the union continue the standoff. Neither side will budge. On the eighth day of the strike, Mr. Stone arrives with several unmarked cardboard boxes. He hands each striker an "I Held the Line" commemorative strike action tee. Another well-timed gimmick.

"Hey, thanks. A free shirt with every strike."

Despite the gimmicks and attempts to boost morale, we are starting to weaken and to lose hope.

"I heard the union boss draws a paycheck over $100,000 and he appointed his wife to a $75,000 consulting job."

"Figures. Jimmy Hoffa would be proud."

On the ninth day, everyone brings their families. Mr. M brings his two girls and I bring Alaska and Caledonia.

"Hey, kiddo, sketch a hopscotch with this sidewalk chalk."

Mr. M's daughter, the bossy sister, grabs the chalk and draws a series of lopsided squares. The striking teachers hop with picket signs on their shoulders. The older sister draws a caricature of her dad, depicting Mr. M with a huge pumpkin-like head.

"That's great."

Inspired, I chalk a portrait of every single teacher on the line, surrounding the school sidewalk. Forty-two portraits. Guardians, sentinels. Ozymandias. I draw Mr. Stone with his stern face; I draw Ms. Fox with a bushy tail. I sketch Ms. W with her bald chemo head.

This high is as temporary as it was necessary and for a while we feel as fresh and ready to confront the administration as the first day of the strike. Like drug addicts, we need more to catch the thrill. School lets out and the children mill around the portraits.

"There's Mr. I."

"There's Ms. W."

"Mr. M has a huge head."

The Principal walks along our line in his 3-piece suit using a walkie-talkie to direct the school buses.

"Who's responsible for this?"

The Principal's a squat, stocky man with a head like a potato. He likes to talk about the fistfights he got into as a ruffian in the Bronx. He values the experiences that shaped him and still thinks of himself as a tough guy. As he studies the drawings, balled-fists at rest on hips, he flicks his nose with his thumb. One of the teachers points at me.

"This is vandalism. We need to call the police."

He turns and marches into the school. The next morning, Mr. Stone, our strike commander, calls me aside.

"An official complaint has been sent to your file."

"How come?"

"It says you hit somebody's car with your sign."

"Really? When?"

The strike has been on for two weeks and we all expect it to settle over the weekend.

"And please, no more antics like the chalk drawings. Did you write 'Scabs' on the entrance to the teacher's parking lot?"

He's shopping me for a scapegoat. I can't understand why someone would lie about me hitting a car until I recall books I've taught in class—*To Kill a Mockingbird*, *The Crucible*, *The Scarlet Letter*…

"This is bullshit. I talked to a cop about the sidewalk chalk, it's legal, protected by the First Amendment, a free speech issue. You can't spit on the sidewalk, the cop said, but drawing on it with chalk is okay. The cop even said, 'It's called sidewalk chalk.'"

That night, it rained. The portraits, like our resolution, faded but remained intact.

Button Pusher

"Hey, Pops, what's going on?"

"How come you never call?"

"I'm calling."

"How's it going, son?"

"Mediocre. The strike's over. I'm tired; my voice hurts. I'm getting a cold, I've got a hundred papers to grade."

"You sound busy. You should take better care of yourself; it seems every time I talk to you, you're sick."

I sip my herbal echinacea tea.

"Did you watch the Grammys?"

"Ah, nope."

"I thought you were into music."

My neck aches.

"I love music. The Grammys are phony. Everyone knows the songs they give awards to are lame. The record companies want so and so to sell a million records, so she wins a Grammy. Charlton Heston won the Spoken Word category with a reading from the Bible. Ridiculous."

"There's nothing ridiculous about the Bible, son."

"It would be equally ridiculous to give a Grammy to the Koran or the Vedas or some Buddhist sutras. The Xtian Bible has nothing to do with Spoken Word. Spoken Word is a genre of poetry where how you deliver your speech carries the same weight as the words you wrote on the page."

"It's better than writing filthy, disgusting things that tear the world down."

"That sounds like the kind of art we need."

"What, are you an atheist?"

"I've been an atheist since I was seven years old and found out that Santa was a damn lie."

"That's no way to raise your family. I feel sorry for your students, they deserve better. You should think about your daughter. Kids today need values. She's hyperactive and undisciplined. We need to teach family values at school. More people should have Christian morality."

"Oh, yeah, like persecuting gays, keeping women barefoot in the kitchen, starting wars across the globe, torturing dissidents, burning witches, turning the other cheek to the murder of six million Jews and collecting tithe so ministers and popes can drive Cadillacs? Name the value our Xtian leaders exhibit with their hands on button to launch a nuclear war. Genocide. Xtians are so ready to rise up into the next world they don't care about this one. They want to bring the apocalypse, so Jesus can visit."

"You need to grow up. When are you going to marry your lady?"

"You've said 'till death do us part' twice. What does marriage have to do with love? We're not getting married until our gay friends can."

"Homosexuality is sick."

"Dad…I…"

"What?"

"Never mind."

There's a pause.

"I don't know how you grew up without knowing any gay people. Your generation kept them in the closet, I guess. I work with people who are 'homosexuals' and they're no sicker than you or I."

"You need to get past this punk phase, son. You should write books you can be proud of. Would you let your daughter read that crap?"

"Of course. Caledonia doesn't need religion to develop a sense of right and wrong. She's a moral being. An original. She's been beyond good and evil from the day she was born. She'll turn out all right as long as I can keep her from the clutches of those damn Xtians."

I hear a door slam in the background and he hangs up the phone.

Nervous Breakdown

Georgie passes something to Fiona.

"Will you please quiet down and get to work?"

I've got a splitting headache.

"Why don't you quiet down, you always picking on us black people, 'cause you don't know how to control your own class."

"Fiona, you need to mind your own business. Please pick up your things and move to this desk in the corner so you can focus on the assignment. We need to respect the rights of others to learn and study."

Stone rules via inimical paroxysms of irrational anger, but I hate yelling. I'm thinking divide and conquer, which worked in some old war movie.

"I'm not moving."

The whole class watches for my next move. It's like a chess game with yelling. I don't plan to blow it, but I'm standing like a ventriloquist dummy. Can no more move, than think.

"Fiona, I need you to sit in Mr. Stone's classroom."

"No sir, I ain't going."

Kids make noises every time I move to speak and talk under my instructions. My head throbs. A cricket-sized simulacrum of every child I've had problems with pounds on my skull. They want out.

"Yes, you are going."

"No, I ain't."

She looks to the class for support. I sense someone making faces behind my back.

"I said get up and get out."

I've lost control. I step into her personal proximity with the intention of helping her out of the seat and toward the door. She resists. My fingers lock around her shirt.

"No."

She holds tight to the desk.

"I said get the fuck out."

I've become that bad cop who whips a blackjack upside the suspect's head after a routine traffic stop. I've become that border patrol agent instructing with a nightstick. This is the cliché straw that breaks the cliché camel—I am crippled and broken.

I see Doctor Pullman in the doorway. He's had it in for me since the first day I came to this school when I called him Mr. Pullman instead of Doctor at a staff development workshop. We nearly bonded while breaking up a fight between a girl and a boy in the hall in front of his classroom. The girl was knocking the crap out of this poor kid who wasn't fighting back. She called him a "fat motherfucker" and was knocking both fists against his body. At the staff development workshop, we discussed school policy in a small group together, but he espies me for an enemy.

"Take your hands off that girl."

My anxiety spins up into a tornado. The room spins too, like vertigo and I might fall into the center of the whirlpool lost to the inhaling abyss. Here is where I snap, where the bending ceases and I break. The student faces press into my indelible memory like pig's teeth stuck in a tree. Julio frowns. Arturo looks perplexed. Stephanie throws contempt. Their expectations about school and how teachers should act uproot. My father, grandpa, Alaska, the whole fucking world tumbles through my hands. The tears bleed down my face and I push past him out of the room.

To my surprise, many students speak in my defense. Students may exhibit signs of Stockholm syndrome, but a cult of personality takes you just so far. Apparently, Doctor Pullman asked Mrs. Chins to watch the class while he informed the Principal. They found me behind the shed at the back of the school where Rosendo got busted for taking a leak. There were cigarette butts pressed into the mud and the faint smell of piss lingered in the air as it does in memory. I sat on a brick wall by the pickleweed, which was flowering. The yellow flowers looked like daisies. The sky was blue and calm.

Mediation

"The rules of this mediation are simple. You listen to the other person without comment."

On Charlene's desk, a half-eaten sandwich rests next to a can of diet soda amidst a jumble of papers. She perches on top of the desk, either to put us at ease or because gazing down from Olympus lends power. I hope she doesn't ask us to shake hands.

It wasn't easy coming back to school this morning. Everyone looks at me differently, like a cancer patient. With the pity they offer Ms. W. People hold you at a distance when you're dying. Fear of contagion or perhaps there are just-so-many seats in the lifeboat.

Around midnight, I wrote this little poem on a napkin at the Ground Zero café.

Now I am the cancer
they will treat me like a disease
cures have little effect on
the other teachers' help, my colleagues
works like chemotherapy, and
in the end when I turn hard and black and
really start to rot within my own skin
they will distance themselves
to protect their own asses—
I wish them well

Fiona sits in a cushioned chair to the right of the social worker. She got her hair done about a week ago, but the braids are starting to unravel. I sit in a similar chair to the left. Fiona has her arms folded across her chest and looks like she might cry.

"Now, Fiona, you said Mr. J discriminates against the black students in class. Could you share your feelings about that?"

She doesn't speak right away. Turns the phrases over in her mind, slowly like a rotisserie chicken, for the best way to lay them out. The social worker bites a sandwich. She has trouble keeping her mouth closed as she chews.

"He's always telling Georgie and me to be quiet, even though other kids talk. Everybody talk in there."

"Okay Fiona, is that it?"

"That's it."

"Mr. J, could you respond?"

"I ask students to be quiet, but… uh… do I tell African Americans more than anyone else? Who did I ask to be quiet before Georgie?"

"Khahn."

"I don't know Khahn, is he black?"

"No. He Chinese."

"Actually, his family comes from Cambodia. Remember when we talked about Nixon secretly bombing Cambodia at the end of the Vietnam War and the refugees… Let me ask you this, are you supposed to be talking in class?"

"No."

"Is there some way I can let you know when you are talking inappropriately that doesn't upset you?"

"I don't know."

"Perhaps some kind of signal. Maybe Mr. J could put his hand on your shoulder."

Charlene puts her hand on my shoulder to demonstrate; it feels creepy.

"I don't want him touching me. I don't want him coming by my desk."

A teardrop rolls from her eye. She could be playing a game—an act to some end beyond my capacity to understand. Or maybe calling someone racist isn't easy. Maybe it's true. Maybe, I am a racist? Maybe I harbor some prejudice I thought I'd risen above? Did they sell me multiculturalism in college or did I believe in it? What of my cosmopolitan sympathies? A true democrat. I climbed out of the melting pot into the salad bowl. I need to review the disciplinary referrals I've written to see if I tolerate more from kids with lighter skin tones. This idea festers inside me. A gradient of faces spread over the floorboards. It seems too big to grapple with. Maybe she has trouble at home. Maybe I remind her of someone who hurt her. In Mr. Stone's class, she's a model student who raises her hand to answer questions.

"Let's meet again tomorrow."

Georgie

The bus ride home from the mountains is relatively quiet, with the kids draped over the seats like road kill, like wet socks hung on the dead branches of dead trees. At Edward Abbey, some parents wait in their cars and others stand in the parking lot. The kids seem anxious to exit the bus.

"Hurry, faggot."

"Quit pushing dick breath."

As I step off the bus, the city air is unremarkable. Kids and parents reacquaint themselves, velvet voices creaking, like returning from a long journey.

"Hola, mija."

"Hi, mom."

"We missed you so much…"

"Put your damn shit in the car."

Many of the children hug their parents; some, uncharacteristically, hug each other.

"Thank you Meester Yonson for bring my mija home."

Loquesha's dad pulls out his wallet and says, "Did she steal or break anything?" After a few minutes, it becomes apparent that a handful of kids need a ride.

Mrs. Kasunic directs a boy from her group to sit in the back seat of her Volvo.

"Do you need a ride home, Arturo?"

"Yeah, Mr. Stone. I guess so cause we ain't got no car."

No one has come to pick up Georgie.

"Don't give that one a ride home."

"Why not?"

"Didn't you read his cumulative file?"

Mrs. Chins speaks in a low voice.

"His father was sent to prison for molesting him."

"That's terrible."

I chuck my sleep roll into my Toyota.

"And he accused his fifth-grade teacher of molesting him, too. The teacher got fired."

"Yeah. Also terrible. I didn't read the file, but it probably says his grandma died last year and he sees her ghost in the halls."

"I know you want to protect him, but you need to let some of them go, for your own survival."

Mrs. Chins stands behind the door to her car, a green Honda.

"Watch yourself."

Alaska and Caledonia are waiting in the Toyota. Georgie paces back and forth.

"Hey, what's the problem?"

"I can't find my damn sleeping bag. Somebody stole it."

"Georgie, who would want your sleeping bag?"

"Hell, if I know."

His arms flail in a gesture I read as frustration. In class, I often catch him staring into space, taking up space—daydreaming. He's failed to turn in most of his assignments. I caught him reading a book once, sort of, if you count searching for the nasty parts in *Waiting to Exhale.*

"Hey, Mr. B. Have you seen Georgie's sleeping bag?"

My voice sounds like I've got emphysema.

"No. We'll look for it Monday."

He's in his Samurai with one of his homeroom students in the passenger seat. He waves.

"Mama's going to whoop my ass."

"It's about time."

His bottom lip folds over the top.

"That's not funny, Mr. J."

"Hey, I didn't take your sleeping bag."

The other boys probably buried it in the woods.

"Did you leave it at the campground?"

The bus trundles from the parking lot; the school is dark.

"I bet Fiona took it."

"It's not here, Georgie. We can ask everyone on Monday."

There's a giant orange ball sunset in the western sky.

"You need a ride?"

He bounces into the back seat next to Caledonia.

"Turn left here."

He directs us down an alley. Alaska put in a full day at work at Ballard's and craves home (shower, couch, food, tv). I drive slowly to avoid potholes; we pass Video Roy's and Jamaica Hut.

"Turn right."

We pass blocks of track houses, which give way to apartments and row houses. Many windows are boarded over with plywood and every vertical surface has been tagged with spray paint.

"Turn right."

"Are you making this up?"

We drive down another unlit alleyway.

"Don't stare at the crack dealer, Cali."

The dude in the alley reaches his hand inside his jacket, wants to look hard and I question why I'm doing this.

"I think it's this way."

"You think?"

"Well, I never had to give directions, we just get in my sister's car and go."

As we pass the Community Actor's Theater, a black Cadillac pulls next to us at the traffic signal. We can't see the driver through the tinted windows.

"Yo, you know where this kid lives?"

We pass Green Cat Liquor and Dashiki Boutique.

"My mom bought a hat there. Turn left."

We enter a more suburban neighborhood. The windows are all covered with iron bars. Georgie points over my shoulder.

"That's Loquesha's house."

I recognize Loquesha's father watering the lawn. He waves.

"Turn right here."

As we pass a block of suburban homes, I notice the patio furniture chained to the front porch.

"Georgie, where do you live?"

He has us driving an unpaved alley, it's muddy, but the potholes don't seem deep enough for us to get stuck.

"You can stop here."

"Here?"

"Yeah, here."

"There isn't a house here."

Georgie hops out and grabs his backpack. He straddles a short fence and cuts around the corner.

"See you later, Georgie."

Alaska and Caledonia wave.

"Bye."

He waves as I maneuver the car out of the alley and turn up the next block.

"Why'd you give him a ride? Let's get out of this neighborhood."

"He's one of my homeroom students, I'm responsible. No worries, this neighborhood isn't any worse than ours."

"We're glad you're back, Daddy."

"I guess we missed you."

"You guess?"

I give Alaska a kiss.

"You feeling better, sweetie?"

"Yes, daddy."

A city bus rolls by bellowing diesel smoke. It's the same #11 I take from my house to school. Skin color changes along the bus route from white to brown to black within thirty minutes as it passes through the segregated city. The lit windows frame solemn black faces on their way home from work.

"Hey, last time I was on this bus, these cats were joking around. One says, 'I benched two-fitty in the joint, you know I'm bulking up, but gotta stop drinking if I'm gonna lose this paunch.'"

I slap my stomach for emphasis.

"'I do 2,000 sit-ups a day, but this belly won't quit me.' His interlocutor said, 'Your woman should be so faithful.' Ha, ha. So, Jack Lalanne gets down in the aisle of the bus and starts doing sit-ups. Ha ha."

Alaska laughs.

As I drive up the street, Georgie skips on the cement toward a beat, old railroad shack. Sometimes I forget my students are still kids; they skip or jump for no reason or burst out in song. The roof sags like it's caving in and a rusty car engine sits in a clump of weeds; there's no light on inside. He pounds on the door and cups his hands on the front window to look in. The shack seems deserted.

Georgie shoulders his backpack and walks away. I pace him up the block.

"He's crying. We should help him."

I roll down the window.

"What's up, Georgie?"

Before he can speak, we all hear a sound like DOOF DOOF DOOF. Gunshots crack on the next block and tires SQUEAL on asphalt.

"What was that?"

"Gunshots."

"Shit, Dan, drive us out of here."

Georgie steps to the car and reaches for the locked passenger door. CH-CH-CH-CH. Sounds like somebody returning fire with an automatic weapon. Caledonia unlocks the door and Georgie jumps in. I drive away fast.

"Thanks, Mr. J. There's nobody at my house and I don't got a key.

He wipes his eyes on his jacket sleeve.

"If you had your sleeping bag, you could camp in the yard."

Alaska slugs me on the shoulder. Caledonia pats Georgie on the back.

"Let's go to our house and eat."

Alaska gives the okay with a slight head nod. When we get home, the phone is RINGING and I run to answer it.

"Hey, Mary, what's up?"

"Stoney wanted me to call you. He got a message from the Principal when he got home that Georgie's mom got arrested. Did you give him a ride?"

"Yeah. He's here."

He looks around our apartment like an Amish adventure in the big city.

"You better call child protective services."

"Um, okay, yeah. We just walked in the door. I'll call you later."

"Daniel…"

Caledonia sets four plates on the table. Alaska made spaghetti with marinara. She pulls one side of her lips back, which I interpret as "we need to talk." I put Billie Holiday on the record player and Charlie Shavers' trumpet pours into the room. Alaska lights candles and sets a bowl of green salad on the table.

"Hey Cali, why did we have you?"

"To get a beer out of the fridge."

"Thanks kiddo."

Alaska motions for me to join her in the kitchen while Georgie and Cali sit down to eat.

"You guys go ahead."

"No prayer?"

Caledonia chortles.

"What's going on?"

She's got an oven mitt on one hand.

"He called his sister, no answer. Mary said Mr. Stone said the Principal said…"

Georgie sops up his sauce with a piece of garlic bread.

"His mom got arrested."

"Arrested? Does he know?"

I shake my head negative.

"He can't stay here."

"Where else can he go?"

"Can I have another bowl, Mrs. J?"

I hand him the pot off the stove and he scrapes the last of it onto his plate.

"You're not going take me to child protective services, are you?"

"Uh… uh, I don't know what to do with you."

Alaska gives me that nod again.

"Don't worry, you can stay until we contact your family."

"Thanks, Mr. and Mrs. J. My mom should be home by now."

He seems like a different kid outside of school. His demeanor is pleasant, even polite.

"Dinner was delicious, Mrs. J; I'll go ahead and wash the dishes."

"Is this the same Georgie Evans from my English class?"

"G Dog, can you read me a bedtime story?"

"Sure Little J. What story you want to hear?"

"The Stinky Cheese Man."

She pulls a dog-eared book from a shelf.

"I'll set up the futon for you."

"What's a Foo-ton?"

"Futon is Japanese for bed-with-no-box-spring."

"Ghetto bed. Don't worry, Mrs. J, I can sleep anywhere, I sleep on the floor at my house."

Georgie must be wondering about his family.

"And the stinky cheese man said, Run, run, run, as fast as you can…"

Caledonia sits on his lap in the rocking chair.

"Time for bed."

Caledonia seems heavier than when I last picked her up. Either that or my muscles are weak from the camping trip. I plant a smooch on her forehead and she reciprocates with a fairy kiss on my cheek as light as air. Caledonia snuggles into the blanket and pulls her stuffed dog tight to her chest.

Georgie excuses himself to go to the bathroom. He's in there a long time and when he comes out, a robust stink follows him down the hall.

"Whoa."

I wave my hand in front of my nose.

"That's worse than yours, Alaska."

She puts one of the candles to a bundle of sage incense.

"You guys smoke, Mr. J?"

"Sorry G Dog, incense."

"I told Cali to call me that. This is cool."

"Thanks. A friend of mine painted it."

"It's like the painting that hangs in class."

"Same artist. You're the first student to notice the art."

He surveys the furniture, the bookshelf. He's like a kitten exploring his new environment.

"*Frisk, Wrong, Try, Naked Lunch*…*Crazy*… *Cock*, Ooooo. Mr. J, what kinda…*Junky, Queer*. Queer? Is that some faggot stuff?"

"Don't say faggot Georgie. Yes, some of these books have gay characters."

"That's sick, Mr. J."

His attention turns to the life drawing of Alaska we had framed. He glances from the drawing over to her and reconciles the clothed and unclothed figures. *La maja desnuda.*

"Oooo, you a nasty family, Mr. and Mrs. J."

Alaska blushes.

Now he's picked up a book of pornographic Greek and Roman art, which I need to return to the library. He flips from the tintinnabulum of erect cocks to an urn with a depiction of a satyr ravaging a maiden to a temple relief of an orgy—a waking eye for every orifice. The book maps positions his adolescent mind hasn't imagined. I sit next to him on the couch and put my hand on his shoulder so I can see the book. The page shows a Roman patrician kissing a young boy.

"This is really sick."

He drops the book on the table.

"It's not the kind of art book you'll see at school."

Georgie walks over to the window. Downtown—banks, hotels, a gray battleship in the harbor. The buildings are older than the ones in his neighborhood but fashioned with more craft. The architecture is sound and the neighborhood is ripe for an unfortunate renaissance. Unfortunate because rents will price us out. The closest tenement has been sprayed with graffiti and boarded up. A couple of really dirty junkies had been squatting, but the cops chased them away. An old brick house sits across the vacant lot and we can see the silhouette of an old woman through a gray, translucent curtain in the upstairs window.

"You like it here?"

"It's cheap."

"I thought teachers made a lot of money."

I should water the browning plants that haven't died yet in the redwood flower box on the patio.

"Mr. Stone rakes it in. He's been teaching for thirty years. I've been teaching full time for two years. Last year we had $88 dollars in the bank."

"Shoot, last year my mama had more than that stuffed under the mattress."

We laugh together for no reason.

"Good night, boys."

Georgie jumps like she startled him. She's wearing a cotton nightshirt and her nipples poke through the thin material. The lassitude in my bones degrades my orbit. I'd like to fall with Alaska into bed and sleep for a thousand years. The thought of her genial warmth relaxes me. Her tender, healing hand. I've got too much work—work the never-ending story, work the overseer, work the bitch, work that omnipresent sore inside my mouth.

"Good night, Mrs. J."

"I need to do some work before I go to bed. I've got papers to grade and have to make a lesson plan for next week."

He sits on the futon and rummages through his backpack for a toothbrush.

"Is it okay if I call my mom again?"

"Uh… uh… Sure, go for it."

I slip Patty Smith's *Dream of Life* on the turntable. Georgie prepares for bed. He's not a fat kid, but he's big, with baby fat cheeks, a smooth chest and a bit of a tummy. His bikini briefs remind me of the Spider-man Underoos I had when I was a kid.

Little blue dreamer, go to sleep, Let's close our eyes and call the deep…

Georgie's putting on the silk pajamas he wore camping. By the time I look up from my paperwork, Georgie's face down in the pillow asleep on the futon.

I'm sitting on the toilet. It's Saturday morning and I'm young enough to remember not thinking about taking a dump. But the feeling inside my bowels becomes more insistent with age.

I woke early and picked up a brown bag of rolls, six for a dollar, at the panadería in Golden Hill. I plan to drink espresso, write in my journal and watch cartoons with Caledonia. *X-men* are on at 9:30. It's a heavy, ponderous crap. After pushing the first log free, I reach for a magazine—an article about the decline in the mammalian sperm count over the last thirty years in North America. Toxins in the air and water cull our kind. They found alligators with small penises in a Florida swamp. *Continued on page 68…* That section has been torn out. I notice a crumpled ball in the trash, hidden under wadded tissues and an earwax-covered Q-tip. I unfurl my missing article. The page sticks to itself with a mild glue.

My own cock hangs dorkily above the water. The second log of shit starts to roll out but explodes as a paint bomb over the inside of the bowl. PLPLPLPTH. Alaska is still asleep. I want to wake her, but she rarely gets a chance to sleep in. My cock grows stiff. I wrap my hand around the ignorant invertebrate.

There's a Calvin Klein underwear model on the back of the article. The young man has a smooth chest and a bit of a tummy. I turn it over to finish reading and stroke until a sharp blast of cum slaps the crumpled paper. I wipe my ass and flush the toilet. I wipe even though I'm jumping straight into the shower.

Georgie sleeps on the futon. He never got under the covers. He presses his face into the pillow just as I left him the night before. I hear the standard rhythmic sounds of sleep and ease the door shut.

He wakes a bit later and sits next to Caledonia on the couch to watch cartoons.

"Did you talk to your sister?"

"Yes, sir."

He stuffs a bite of roll in his mouth.

"Rye rom rin rail."

"Mmm."

He gets up from the couch and walks out onto the patio. I sip espresso from my favorite cup.

"Is he going to be okay?"

"I'm not sure, sweetheart."

"Are you going to jail, Daddy?"

"I hope not."

I step into the morning sunlight and find Georgie staring vacantly into the vacant lot. It doesn't seem fair. The sun glistens on the still bay water. I wish I had some wisdom to help him through the tangled congeries of thought. What would Stone say? Chins? Gandhi? Tolstoy? Angela Davis taught me to hate prison. I hear a faint mumble.

"Run run run, as fast as you can. You can't catch me, I'm the stinky cheese man.

Part II: Where Different Rules Apply

Invocation to a Riot

Enter a bloodshot eye. My voice has crapped out—the vocal
cords twang like a breaking G string on Woody Guthrie's guitar. I should teach sign language. I've used my sick days; the
school gave them to me to use when I was sick, so I did. A few
of my colleagues don't like this. Maybe they never get sick or
all the dumb diseases they've had over the years have built robust immune responses. Last night for homework, I asked the
kids to describe their bowel movements.

> Ex. 1: Three seals huddling in brown bay water.
>
> Ex. 2: The spire of a church rising to the noonday sun.

By the size of the stack of papers in the inbox, everyone did the
homework. Oh, regular youth. I can't talk, so let the VCR
teach. It's the end of the school year and a lot of teachers are
showing movies. Mrs. Chins showed *The Bridges of Madison
County* and I'm showing Russ Meyer's *Supervixens*. A robot could
do it. But I can't keep the class quiet. Kids talk to each other,
fail to pay attention, look bored and ignore my suggestion to
take notes for a quiz. Any flak from the parents, at this point, is
irrelevant. I'll argue my right to show Russ Meyer films in
front of the Supreme Court. I'd like to sit with Ruth Bader
Ginsberg and Clarence Thomas as they watch *Mudhoney* and
Faster, Pussycat! Kill! Kill!

I spent last week on jury duty. The first case was murder.
Watching the lawyers interview jurists during voir dire was
better entertainment than prime-time tv.

"Could you shed some light on the misdemeanor charge in 1976, Mz. Hays?"

"Mmmrrrmmm."

"A little louder, please."

"I was picked up for soliciting."

Mz. Hays reminded me of my grandma. She let her head fall limp and I wondered who was on trial. The next woman got the same treatment.

"Were you ever the victim of a crime?"

"I was raped."

"We need more details, miss."

"Three times."

"Could you elaborate?"

"Uh... um, I, uh. It hurt... It hurt a lot. Each time."

"Mrs. Butler, were you assaulted by a military serviceman?"

I suppose they had to ask these questions because a Marine Corps corporal was accused of shaking his newborn baby to death.

"Georgie, will you please be quiet, please? We're trying to watch this movie."

He points out the window.

"But Mr. J, look, there goes my granny."

He points at a woman carrying a tray of lumpia to the sixth-grade classroom. Georgie sees his dead grandmother all the time. She'd been the only stable person in his life and when she died his will to do school work died too. They let him pass the sixth grade after summer school.

"Let's watch the movie, please."

Most of the kids want to please their teacher and turn back to the film. It's the scene where SuperEula rides in the dune buggy. Before I became a full-time middle school English teacher, a history teacher told me not to show movies because the kids play with themselves in the dark. He said he was always wiping jism from the desks after class. Old hacks may haze the newbies—I haven't seen any errant jizz.

After his mom got locked up, Georgie ended up living with his sister and nephew. He's found a new way to compel attention by tossing up the sign for West Side. He came to school with a blue bandanna around his forehead and dark sunglasses and someone yelled, "Take that rag off, faggot" in the hall.

"You'd better give me the costume, Georgie."

"Why, Mr. J?"

"I'll give you two reasons, G-dog. One, because gang-affiliated clothing violates school policy and two, some fool is gonna pop a cap in yo ass."

When the Principal called me into his office yesterday, I didn't expect him to fire me. I knew things were bad, but thought I had improved.

"Dan, we're not going to renew your contract for next year. Teaching is a dichotomy of charisma and pedagogy. Your classroom management has improved, but not enough to meet the team's expectations."

There's a bit of silence and I don't know if my mouth is hanging open or closed.

"One thing I noticed while observing your class was that the students changed their posture when I walked into the room."

Wesley had yelled, "The Principal's coming," which caused the whole group to sit up in their chairs—I adjusted my posture too. He proceeded to tell the class that their teacher was a poet and then, to show that he was a poet too, recited, "There was an old woman who swallowed a fly…" He ran right through the barnyard, stanza on stanza, cats, dogs, pigs, until she'd swallowed a fucking horse. I can't say what my posture was doing at that point.

The Principal stood up and I felt immediately intimidated by his single-mindedness. He had his shirt sleeves rolled to the elbows, a yellow stain in the pits and bags under his eyes. The rumor was he sometimes stayed at school thirty-two hours straight. A little white powder coated his lip, probably from a donut. He shook my hand and slapped me on the back.

The other case on jury duty was wrongful termination. I didn't make the final twelve on that one either, so gleaned no advice to help myself. I wanted to rat the team out for every infraction, proclaim that my class learned more than Mrs. Chins'— barking at and basing on students. I wanted to say that the team controls kids by yelling. And that I don't yell. I wanted to whine, complain, beg, rationalize and make excuses because Alaska shouldn't go another year without new clothes. Caledonia shouldn't go a day without medical benefits. I don't care about appliances or safe cars or owning a home.

"Stop it Fiona."

I scan the room for the voice disturbing our movie again.

"Georgie, be quiet. Do you want to end up in prison like your mama?"

That was a mistake, even though it worked and he's quiet. A silence fell across the whole room. Fiona, however, flies out of her seat, nearly pushing the desk over. Our truce is broken.

"You can't talk to him like that."

I reach for my water glass, take a drink, which burns the back of my throat.

"Shut your dumb ass up, no one asked you to speak."

Her mouth falls open.

"I'm telling my daddy on you and he gonna come down here and bust yo nut."

I sip from my glass and wipe my lips with one hand.

"Yeah right, when your mama finds out who he is maybe he can teach you ignorant fucks how to read."

My vocal cords are numb; I've moved beyond pain.

The whole class erupts like a volcano—goes crazy. Juan writes "1, 2 FUCK SCHOOL" on the front board in his signature tag. Fiona slings the desk to the corner which CLATTERS and lands legs up. Arturo snaps awake, comes up swinging and sticks the first punch on Georgie's nose. A shocking amount of blood hits the linoleum. Georgie screams. Two girls who'd been mad doggin each other all year pull hair and scream obscenities.

"Fuck you island-nigger bitch."

The last time two girls fought at school, one of them got her shirt ripped off and the other lost part of an ear. Fiona moves toward me with a box cutter. I hear pages being ripped from lit books and school supplies flying all around the room.

Some of the kids are wearing the coatimundi, white-tailed deer, squirrel spirit and jaguar masks we made for the final project of our unit on the Maya.

Mrs. Chins storms into the room.

"What the fuck's going on?"

A few boys from her class jump into the melee.

"Smash it up."

My water glass breaks against the back wall like a SHOT. The fight reminds me of the dance floor at The Bacchanal, second time around for The Damned's "Last Show Ever." No idea why old punk bands threaten to retire. There's no pension, no Old Punks' Home and no chance of being fit for real work. Here's

Wattie from The Exploited working in a bank with a red mohawk and a T-shirt that says, "Let's Start a War."

A yellow flash catches my eye as Oscar sets the homework he never turned in on fire with a Zippo lighter. More glass breaks as the windows fall. Everybody screams.

"Waz up now, Cuz?"

Arturo swings at anybody in range. Vomit Boy takes a hard knock and doubles over clutching his guts. Before Fiona can cut me, Arturo grabs her by the hair and swings her to the floor.

"Stop this. Stop this."

Mrs. Kasunic stands near the door, like Security Staff at The Bacchanal guarding the stage against crowd surfers. She gets pulled into the pit and I lose sight of her in a cartoon blur of legs, feet and fists. The fire alarm rings and the automated sprinkler system kicks into action, like a firefighter hosing down a protest march. The entire school pours into the hallway.

"Okay kiddies, don't panic, file out in an orderly manner."

My vocal cords are useless and lend no sound to my mock instructions. There's a torrent of wet blood and mucus streaming across the floor. That little kid, Roger, kicks Mrs. K like a soccer ball. Vomit Boy's turbid puke overflows the fingers covering his mouth.

Georgie drags Mr. Blythe into the back room and Fiona's weave is on fire. Her screams rise over the tumult.

"Stop, drop and roll."

There's still no voice in my voice. She smells like burning rubber. I fight my way to the back, step over bodies and broken
furniture. The room fills with smoke, but the fight goes on and
on. Juan tries to steal the VCR, gives up and stuffs the tape in
his khaki Dickies. He escapes along the edge of the fisticuffs.
I'm at the door to the back room. Mr. Blythe lies face-down on
the floor, a trickle of blood squeaks from his nose. His eyes shut
like a refrigerator light going out. Georgie lies on top of him
with pants around his ankles. He's wearing black bikini briefs
and says, "Run, run, run…" in a voice that sounds like an alarm
clock wound too tight. I shut the door.

Across the room, a shadowy figure stands in the doorway. It's
Mr. Stone. You can tell by the blazing corona about his head.

"Please stop all this madness…..Stop!"

Mr. Stone lives in the moment of the eclipse and steps outside
of time. His voice penetrates everything. The classroom falls silent. The fire goes out. The smoke clears.

A Plague of Boils

"Active people go to the beach, swim, hike."

I watch Alaska place four small pieces of frozen banana, two frozen strawberries, a heaping cup of frozen cherries and a fistful of fresh spinach into a blender with hemp, chia, flax, turmeric, cayenne, nutmeg, cinnamon and crushed ice.

"Let's start by hiking around Cuyamaca on Saturday. We'll play all day, sleep all night."

"Um, uh… I prefer to stay up late into the night drinking at home or at the bar."

I shouldn't need to remind her of my desperate fear of the Cuyamaca Wolf Spider.

"Our family needs quality time…"

I push the pillow into my face to shut out the evil brightness. My hangover head throbs. My right eye flutters with some kind of spasm. I can't go to the wilderness for exercise. Exercise should be an integral part of daily life. Don't go for a walk; walk to the grocery store. I'd rather dig a ditch or unload trucks or swing an axe.

"We got a bottle of tequila; everything is under control."

I've been physically ill for so long, I can't remember health. It's like a forgotten mood I matured out of. Some serious men, who I pegged as the school district's Psychological Trauma Squad Detail, spoke with some of my students. They came to mop up the psychic blood. (The Building Services Supervisor mopped up the actual blood.) I feel partially responsible. My union rep tied up the loose ends, but I don't remember much. No charges would be pursued if I agreed to never teach again within the sovereign borders of California.

"Jesus Jimmy, I know you're sick, don't leave reminders on the wall of the shower."

"Sorry honey, won't let it happen again. But the shower is the perfect place to eject phlegm from your system and if you don't shoot those bloody boogers at the wall, they cling to your pubes."

A few days later, we replay the same argument and I posit the same rationale for shooting snot on the shower wall… and offer the same apology.

This is about the time the unsightly blemishes appear on my face. Red sores mark the corners of my lips, giving me a clown-like smile. I don't know if they're the stumps of ingrown facial hair or some kind of social disease. A pox maybe. The underside of my nose resembles a baboon's asshole.

"You look like shit."

"Thanks, Cecil. Have you ever been aware of the lymph glands in your throat?"

"Drink more water."

My dad's voice is starting to sound old over the telephone. Our medical insurance was revoked when I lost the job, and now that there's time to stay home sick, I can't afford to.

"I read in a magazine that green snot means you're contagious, so don't breathe on anyone."

I paste the dirty tissues into a notebook so we can catalog the phase in phlegm color. When my voice goes dark like a transformer box hit by a drunk driver, I try to sleep. Minutes? Days? Periods?

Gylan Kain of The Last Poets said, "Time ain't real no how."

On the day I go to clean out my personal belongings, I find Arturo, Juan and Oscar hanging around the school.

"What gives, guys? School's out and you come to class."

"Yo, Mr. J, can we help?"

"We?"

"Shut up, Booster."

"Sure Arturo, cool. Hey, take my classroom key. You never know when you might need to open a certain door. Keep a ring of keys and label them."

The most effective learning has real-life applications. The boys grope through the burnt and twisted ruins for salvage. It's a box of broken crayons. SF McBean's painting survived, but someone scribbled a girl's name on it.

"Yeah, put that in my car. At the beginning of the year, I had eight packs of markers which I bought with my own money. And now I've got half of two packs. What's so funny?"

"I bet Mrs. K has every single marker."

Mrs. Kasunic's strength was keeping her things in order. She made me sign a checkout sheet and deposit my driver license to borrow her scissors.

"At least I'm not lying in intensive care."

"You're funny, Maestro."

Juan looks surprised when I hand him his uncle's magazine.

"I'll see you guys around."

"Thanks, Mr. J."

Most of the supplies in my room were destroyed. The Building Services Supervisor reads *The Wall Street Journal* at his desk in the stock room and doesn't acknowledge my presence, so I take a ream of computer paper off the shelf to run through my printer at home. I fill my satchel with staples, paper clips, tacks, brads, red and black ink pens, writing journals, hanging file folders, construction paper, glue sticks and a container of those tiny adhesive rings that keep your 3-ring binder paper from ripping out at the holes. I would love to top the sundae with Mrs. Kasunic's scissors.

I poke my head into Room 42, where Ms. F finishes her year-end chores. Seeing her reminds me of the after-school mixer at

Hughson's Tavern on Shelter Island. The Principal drank five straight shots of tequila and Ms. F lost one of her shoes.

I pile the two fluorescent light fixtures from my room into my car and three wrap-around desks to use as patio furniture. I slip Mrs. Chins' PMS B-I-T-C-H coffee mug into my magic satchel. The Apple computers in Mrs. Tekhne's room are bolted to the table, but an ink cartridge for a laser printer finds its way into the sack. Instead of hiding the keys to the file cabinet, I rock-walk it to the car like one of those sculptures on Easter Island. I toss 150 report cards into the recycling bin on the way out.

I end by urinating behind the shed where I had a good cry. It's an incredible piss that keeps streaming out of me. It might not stop; I might piss the whole summer away right here. After a long minute, I shake the last drops and zip up my trousers.

As I trundle out of the parking lot with my Toyota loaded to maximum capacity, June 15th marks the first free morning since I became a teacher.

A few hours later, I decide to celebrate my jubilee with Cecil Hayduke at the bag, the box, the bar called Live Wire.

"Another pint of the black should stop up that runny nose."

"Thanks, mate."

It's too loud to carry conversation. Cheap Trick plays on the jukebox.

> *Mommy's all right, Daddy's all right, they just seem a little weird...*

I step up to play the first ball of The Jazz Dynasty and replace the high score with an all-time 1,678,400,000—impossible never before seen. If I hit the magician's trunk in the middle of the play field four more times, the machine will reveal its last secret.

"Shit."

"Give him another, barkeep. Hey, Jazz, I got this theory. You can talk to girls in this bar with your pants down and they won't notice."

"Why not?"

"Cause they always look into your eyes."

When things heat up in the bar—as the jukebox plays three good songs in a row and we approach a moment of peak drunkenness, the hustlers stop shooting pool because too many bodies have crowded around the table and the barback scouts for empty glasses to wash. Somehow, I remember to look down, and sure enough, six guys stand with Levi's 501s bunched around their ankles.

The next morning, the gargoyle masks of Spanish colonialism stare down on me from the architectural façade of the Casa Del Prado Theater in Balboa Park. I'm waiting in a long line of parents, siblings and grandparents with a good measure of aunts, uncles and friends of the family. It's the bi-annual Dance Recital and Caledonia is one of twenty tap dancers tapping CLACK, CLACK, CLACK. I can't stand the music they play, so I brought a

Bad Religion tape. Proud daddy and punk rocker. My boots are laced up for kicks and my T-shirt says Bad Religion too.

A flock of tourists gawk, point, whisper.

"My god. What's wrong with that strange man? Never the likes in Mason City."

I took a vow on my wine-stained prayer carpet this morning to wear a pirate's eye patch for an entire week. My eye twitches underneath. Seekers may fast while others bargain with celibacy or silence.

"Hey, buddy. Did I clown the way you dress? Whatchu looking at me Arty? Arrggh. *Go to hell with Superman and die like a champion, yeah hey.*"

The man in line behind me stares at a pigeon roosting under the eaves. He's spent his whole life avoiding confrontation and sees no reason to step in the middle of anything.

After the performance, Alaska and Caledonia go home and I go to the bar with Cecil. We drink at a table in the corner.

"Hey, Jazz, I gotta ask you something."

"No no. First, I gotta tell you how great little Caledonia's dance performance was today. She was tapping out stardust under the bright stage lamps. It was beautiful. None of these girls were Savion Glover, but they tapped those tiny shoes in unison— right foot eight times, left foot eight times. Of course, when they were supposed to turn to the left, a few got mixed up and bumped into each other. It was great. After they left the stage, the fifty-to-seventy-year-old class emerged from the wings wearing spandex leotards and ended their waltz high-kicking. One of the dancers was four hundred pounds; he was incredible."

Cecil sips his pint.

"He had a pink leotard. He was fearless and not a bad dancer. Made me want to take some classes."

I sip my ale.

"The crappy music couldn't touch me as the Walkman retained battery power through the entire three-hour show. *People out there say I'm no good, 'cause I don't believe the things that I should...*"

Cecil's gaze moves around the room. He's thinking about that next drink or pinball or about picking up chicks.

"Some rich broad wearing a diamond necklace and a velour tracksuit tapped my shoulder and said, 'Could you turn that down, please?' I glared at her with my eye patch—"

"What's with all these sores on your face?"

"Fuck. A plague of boils. Perhaps the gods are punishing me for my sins."

"I thought you didn't believe in sin."

"I don't believe in the gods either."

Cecil gestures with his Belushi-brow that someone worth looking at has entered the bar.

Time Killing Machine

"Dan? Dan, are you listening to me?"

She waves her hand in front of my face checking for stupefaction but my eyelids don't blink.

"I don't know anyone named Dan. Dan?"

"Jimmy, let's walk on the beach. We need exercise."

"Let's spend some quality time together, babe. I rented videos. I got *Total Eclipse* and *Basketball Diaries.* A DiCaprio Fest. Don't you want to know how the French symbolist poet Arthur Rimbaud was able to quit writing?"

"Is Sylvester Stallone in this?"

"I don't think so."

"What's a cymbalist?"

"Somebody who… symbolizes."

"Maybe you should quit writing."

"Yeah, but I don't know how. Maybe DiCaprio will divulge the secret. I'm the poet of the know-its, but quitting stuff appeals to my ascetic side."

I put the movie into the VCR and mount the couch with a bottle of wine in each hand while Alaska makes popcorn. I pass one of the bottles and we share our snack from the same bowl. For the same reason that Rimbaud, in the film, couldn't listen to a poet "butcher French poetry," we couldn't watch the film. I'm not saying the film was shit. Let's say there are times for reading books and watching tv and times for adventure. I began to run my fingers through Alaska's black hair and she leaned in to kiss me.

There was a scene in the film where Verlaine set his wife's tresses ablaze. So, after the movie, I pulled the curtain closed and lit a wax taper.

"Don't come near me with that."

"Come on, babe. Verlaine lit his wife on fire."

"Verlaine also shot Rambo."

"Ha ha."

"Let's make a little love, do a little dance."

"You might try a different aphrodisiac. Maybe Cecil Verlaine will take it up the ass."

"A lawyer by trade, Cecil is more likely to give it to me up the ass."

"You know, Dan or Jimmy the Poet, you should pull a Rimbaud. Start by burning all those nasty poems in the sea chest…"

She takes up the brassy candelabrum by its torso and moves *s'élancer en avant* toward the trunk containing my complete works. I pick up a kitchen knife, joking if she's joking. The flame, shaken, rights itself.

"These are nothing a fire can't fix."

"Please. Those poems are my thoughts. You can't burn a man's thoughts. Burn my body instead. Come on baby, light me on fire. Those poems in the trunk rival the verses of Emily Dickinson and Donna Juarez."

"Who's Donna Juarez?"

"Nobody knows. Her poems never made it out of the trunk."

She laughs and I exhale. I'm not sure how close we came to sublime conflagration. Burn the poems, burn the house, burn the city. She plops on the trunk and I long to lean into her for support—but she seems so far away.

"If I get famous, someone will want to read the journals and letters and little poems."

"You better start eating healthy and exercising. If you die first, I'm burning them."

"Kafka asked Max Brod to burn his poems. He couldn't do it because burning a friend's poems is like burning a friend. You're a consumer, capitalism changes humiliation into money. This is your best shot."

I sit next to her.

"You need to brush your teeth before you kiss me."

"Do you think Rimbaud brushed his teeth?"

"And shave that face, the stubble irritates my skin."

"I'm trying to save the environment by forsaking razors. All that plastic ends up in the sea."

I go into the kitchen thinking that if she loved me, if any true passion ran like a firestorm through her loins, she wouldn't allow body odors or stubble to bar my embrace.

"Fuck."

I throw the knife to stick it in the wall, its CLATTER echoes from the floor through the hollow house. I open the refrigerator, but there's not much in it. I'm not hungry for food, so I close it. The idea of loving someone who doesn't feel passion feels so repugnant that I need to stockpile courage to face her.

"Dan, are you going to search for a new job before your unemployment checks run out?"

I don't acknowledge her question because she used Dan again, a name I no longer recognize.

"We'll need more dollar bills in the bank account to rent movies for the remaining days of our lives."

"We'll switch to free tv like the normal folks."

Sometimes my own thoughts chill me to the bone.

A Parable of Madness

It's been a rough week. First, our car got stolen. The cops said they found an abandoned vehicle of the same model near our apartment. Maybe there was something wrong with the first one. Maybe it was out of gas. Maybe this car is just easy to steal. The cops offered no speculation and scant hope of recovery. That very same day, Alaska got fired for giving a cup of coffee to Helen Van Schaack, who had offered her a ride home. Helen worked in the lingerie department. The manager accused Alaska of theft and called it a "slippery slope" which, unaddressed, would lead to employees wearing the shoes home at night or borrowing lacy underthings for hot dates.

So now we're both unemployed.

Helen had gotten romantically involved with Matt, the store Security Chief. (She was fucking him.) While sharing an illicit kiss in the stockroom between pallets of shoe boxes stacked over their heads, he tasted coffee in her saliva. She told him Alaska gave her an espresso drink and he carried this information straight to management. Matt, the store Security Chief had been screwing seven different girls in the store and gotten one pregnant. Unfortunately for Helen, the gossip about his promiscuity was slow-moving and none of the girls seemed to know about the others. Helen was aware he had to catch x number of employees per month, aware of his quota, but sacking Alaska over a coffee seemed beyond the pale. Caught between sex and friendship—Helen chose Matt.

What galled me was seeing Alaska reduced to an "x number." One day you're Employee of the Month, the next you're on the dole.

"Did you give Helen a cup of coffee?"

"Yes."

"Did she pay for it?"

"No."

"I'm sorry, but we have to let you go."

Three years of hard work, several commendations for customer service and a lot of sweat evaporates in a royal "we."

"Proof you should never work."

Helen moonlights as a stripper at The Pair O' Dice and Cecil heard they had a five-ball machine, so we decided to check it out. I pushed through the heavy leather flap hanging over the doorway and the smell of stale bar yeast and dry urine filled our nostrils. The place had lost its liquor license after the bartender served a minor. Forced to sell soda pop, Management told the girls that if they wanted to keep working, the place was going all nude. Helen shook her naked ass for tips under a flashing disco ball. She had long legs and long breasts like tennis balls in wet socks.

I'd met Helen a few times at the store on my way to pick up Alaska after her shift. It's weird when you know the stripper, even a little. Like your nephew stepping up to the plate at a ball game or a friend playing guitar in a local band. You're a spectator but not just a spectator.

Alaska would never take her clothes off in public. Helen's big hips swayed, as a tattooed flame burned up one leg to a freckled buttock.

"There are fourteen silver rings."

I leaned over Cecil's shoulder as he played his last ball to fluster him with this information. The ball drained and he pushed the machine too hard. When the tilt mechanism cut off the points he earned at play, he yelled, "Shit."

"You got your pay docked by the pinball god."

I pulled the plunger and pushed the ball in play for my turn. I hit the ball up the left ramp and smacked it up the right ramp with the next shot. Special was lit. One more loop and I had a free game. Cecil leaned in close.

"There are fifteen, man. Fifteen rings."

He pushed a wet finger into my ear but I made the shot and the machine delivered a satisfying CLOK! The action on the old five-ball machine was slow, so we left the free game for the next player and watched Helen dance.

Cecil tipped a single, tucked into the garter that cut her fleshy thigh. He raised his eyebrow, so I'd note the needle tracks behind her knee. She wheeled her butt around in his face and her breasts swung like pendulums. A beer-swiller with tousled hair in a cheap suit held up a dollar bill and she pranced across the stage to collect.

We decided to wait in the car and play our own music. Cecil put on RL Burnside and passed the flask. After about an hour, Matt, the Security Chief came to pick her up. Before she even had her seatbelt on, he put his hand out for the money. She gave him a stack of ones and he gave her a little bag of dope.

Later that week, Alaska and I run into Helen in front of Granny's Lounge. She looks different in street clothes. She's with a guy who isn't Matt, the Security Chief. He seems as anxious to exit as I am to enter the bar for a drink.

"Hi, Alaska."

"Hi, Helen."

"How's it going?"

"Good, how's it going?"

"Good. I didn't know you hung out at Granny's?"

"Ya, you know. If you're going in, watch out for Madness."

"Uh… okay."

Inside the bar, a few vodka-tipplers sit nailed to their stools along the bar and a married couple sip strong wine at a booth by the window. The ambient light comes from the jukebox and a Miller High Life sign above the taps. Alaska sits on a cozy loveseat near the window and I order two pints of the black at the bar. On my return, some guy is sitting next to her. There's not much room, but I wedge myself in, using my elbows. I hand Alaska her pint and we clink glasses.

"This is Madness."

"I can see that."

"They call me Madness 'cause I like madness bands."

His breath stinks. He's unstable, wobbly, pished. I take a long drag at the pint. Shoving the glass in his face would be a waste of finely crafted stout—so I drain the pint in a sip.

"I hate the color of your socks and shoes, dude."

No one has inspected my socks since Wesley. I check the bar and half-expect the students to jump out and yell, "Surprise." I lift one red Chuck Taylor off the ground for inspection.

"They look gay."

"You wanna fuck my shoes?"

He doesn't respond.

"Hey, look at this."

Alaska opens her purse and pulls out pictures of our daughter.

"This is from her dance recital…"

"Oh, for cute. Your shoes are still stupid, man."

"I don't give a shit about shoes. Shoes mean nothing. Shoes haven't had meaning in years. Sure, I used to check out shoes from across the room. 'Dig those kicks—one of us, one of us.' They sell the shoes you're wearing at Ballard's. Rich people buy them. Consumers. The good old days of cool shoes are dead."

"My boyfriend is Jimmy Jazz. Have you heard of him, Mr. Madness?"

"Fuck no."

"He's a poet. He writes really great poetry."

The glass warms in my palm and a shot of adrenaline goads my heart to pick up the pace and send oxygen to eyes, muscles, fists… It's fight or flight.

"I work in the tool room at the shipyard."

He speaks with a fading Minnesota patois.

"I been in jail twice."

His tough exterior is starting to melt, become softer, more beaten and pathetic.

"Uff-d, I spent the day in court. I don't fucking give a shit."

"Last call for happy hour."

"Last call for freedom of speech."

The barkeep shouts over Martha & the Vandellas blaring out of the jukebox.

They're dancing in Chicago, down in New Orleans…

I step to the bar and purchase two more pints. With a pint in each hand, I see Alaska's arms around Madness. She holds him like the son she always wanted and lays a healing hand on his shoulder. A single tear runs down his face onto her shoulder.

"He needed to be touched. Either I hugged or you slugged."

El Maestro's Gang

We ride down Texas Street into Mission Valley. A steep and narrow pass cuts through the chaparral and sagebrush that line the canyon, cultivated to stem erosion and protect the houses at the rim. Barrel cactus, yucca and an occasional Mexican fan palm accent the landscape. Arturo, Juan and Arturo's cousin Hector bounce around in the truck bed under the camper shell. Arturo leans on the spare tire with his elbow. Cousin Hector sits very still. He's older than the other boys and plagued by an awareness of consequences. I don't know his background, only that he's vigilant and ready for anything. He doesn't say much—doesn't complain. Juan, of course, grumbles throughout the ride despite Arturo telling him to shut up in Spanish.

"Callate la boca, Booster."

From the shotgun seat, I can see the dark line of trees that demarcates the river, which trickles into the Pacific at Dog Beach. The I-805 freeway overpass spans the valley above. The air is crisp, the evening cloudless and shows a few stars since the marine layer peeled back out to sea. I recognize the Big Dipper.

"How much longer till we get there, Mr. J?"

"Quit whining culo, we're here until we get there. And quit farting; that shit's not funny."

Jack Murphy Stadium sits dark to the east, leaving a strip-mall as the only well-lit destination. There's a craft store, a Radio Shack, a car wash, a discount clothier in addition to the Ballard's where Alaska used to work. The marquee of the Valley

Circle Theatre advertises a film called *Dangerous Minds*. The theater's brutalist wings make it look like a cement monument to a modernist spaceship. I saw *Star Wars* here when I was in sixth grade. A field trip with the Safety Patrol—four hundred kids in white uniforms delivered a choral "BOO" when Darth Vader appeared on screen. Luke wore white; Vader wore black. It was easy. I saw the movie nine more times. In simpler days, they trained us to divide the world into good and bad, a Manichean duality of right and wrong. They told us about a struggle between good and evil where we were good and they were evil. The *Star Wars* saga grew more complicated and so did our understanding of the world. Even when people seem to be ineradicable shits, with some effort you can bore, drill down into it and unearth power, privilege, abuse; work-stress oxidizes layer by layer and is hard to strip off.

My guts churn with apprehension. Cecil changes the radio and catches Lou Reed.

Alright! And it was alright…

If we weren't pessimistic materialists, we might take Lou Reed's proclamation as an omen. He's right though, everything's going to be alright. Near closing on a Tuesday, the managers minimally staff the store. Your average consumer will be at home watching prime-time tv so it won't be crowded. We keep our eyes open for the unlikely hero, the man who saw too many cowboy movies—like *Star Wars*.

I'd dialed Arturo's number so many times I knew it rote, but last night was the first I asked to speak to him rather than his mother. I had told his mother that he was headed down the wrong path and that by working together, we could save him. I believed that. His mother humored me, played along. She knew he was on the wrong path because so was she. They lived on the wrong path. I thought his criminal bravado was an act, that he was smart enough to go to college and that my job was to push him in that direction—he figured he was smart enough to stave off jail and make a good run. Arturo carried this determinism around. He recognized his limitations and was determined to enjoy life while the party lasted. Teachers want to show kids a way out and maybe they can. At this moment, I'm actually driving him down the wrong path.

I'd given him a ride home once, so I knew to pick him up at an apartment complex in Encanto. There weren't enough trees in this neighborhood, just power lines, yelling neighbors and graffiti. His mother stayed by the window that time I dropped him off, wringing her hands. His stepfather stood over the stove, frying carnitas on a high flame. The man's neck was covered with faded tattoos. He wore a thick mustache and allowed a lit cigarette to waver over their supper. Arturo intimated in class discussion that he didn't respect the man, especially when his "step" was drunk. You catch pieces of kids' lives. The stepfather had been drinking before my visit; the party moving at pace for several days had reached an apotheosis. Loaded ashtrays and Modelo empties competed with intricate layers of food smells. A strange woman sat cross-legged on the floor. She didn't say anything and no one paid any attention to her. Aunt? Sister? Neighbor? Roommate? The last victim of Jonestown clutching a bible and staring at the tv. A transistor radio played cumbias in the kitchen and the rhythm influenced the way the stepfather flipped the meat around in the pan.

"Hey, Arturo."

"Hola, Mr. J? ¿Qué pasa Maestro? Uh… what are you callin… about that essay, it's too late. Just give me a D on it, so I can dodge summer school. I got stuff to do this summer. You know?"

"Don't worry, Arturo; I gave you an A in my class. An A for academics and an F for citizenship. You're no citizen."

"Cool."

"Listen, Arturo. I want to put a gang together."

I expected mockery, but all I could hear was music in cacophony with the sound effects from a tv cop show. He seemed to listen to my proposition, listening more intentionally than in class—though a teacher doesn't always know when they're tuned in. Kids will surprise you and repeat your words. I told him about the shoe store, about Alaska being terminated. I described the rat-fink Security Chief and his rat-fink girlfriend with such vivid detail that I was sure Arturo could pick them out of a lineup.

"Seriously, I want to put a gang together, like Pancho Villa."

"Pancho Villa?"

"Ya."

"Okay, Maestro. I'll bring my cousin Hector and call that pinche pendejo Juan Maldonado from class."

I wasn't excited about having Juan in the gang, but Arturo swore he was a talented thief, which reminded me that Juan had given an oral presentation on shoplifting in class. I'd given him a C because he didn't make eye contact with the audience, nor did he bring the required visual aid.

"If he's going to steal with us, he needs to wash his hands. My grandfather worked with his hands. He took meticulous care of his nails. They were always clean…"

Cecil wants to smoke before we go in. He guides the truck into the shadows close to the store entrance. The vast parking lot is nearly empty; a few cars are parked under pools of yellow light. Cecil takes a drag from the pipe he keeps loaded in the glove box, which triggers a violent coughing fit, attributable, he says, to a small lung capacity. His face moves through a gradient from red to purple. Fate could save our asses with a trip to the emergency room. I take the pipe from his twitching hand and pass it through the sliding-rear-glass. The cab reeks of weed. Hector waves it off. Arturo and Juan study me harder than any test I gave in class. Juan hits the pipe with a lighter from his khaki Dickies. This is also a test. Arturo waits for my reaction, but my attention is focused on the store.

"Don't blow that shit at me, I got probation."

Cecil HACKS as the boys climb out of the truck and lights a cigarette.

"They got snacks in here? I'm hungry."

"Shut up, Booster. You act like you never been out of the ghetto. This place has sharp threads, you got to be pimpin' to afford this shit."

"I got these shoes on clearance. Even with Alaska's discount, they cost forty bucks."

Pancho Villa wouldn't wear $40 shoes. I want to suggest we go for frozen yogurt or take in the movie. Arturo swaggers with his chest out and Juan doesn't seem capable of walking a straight line. Arturo's cousin Hector stays off to the side in the shadows.

"Should I give a pep talk before we go in? Do we need a plan?"

"Naw, man, just fuck shit up."

As clear an articulation of our guiding principle as any. I hold the glass door for the boys. Cecil takes a last drag and flicks the cigarette away. Its smoldering tip explodes in sparks against the front display window. It feels like we're being watched.

I remember picking up Alaska once with SF McBean and this junkie-kid we called Puzzlebox. The kid had blue hair and "100 Punks Rule" painted on his leather. That was the same night Sam Kinison tried on sweaters in the aisle with his entourage. Alaska pointed out the narcs that tracked our movements through the store. She also said not to worry about surveillance cameras because the bosses trained them on the registers to monitor employee theft.

Arturo's cousin Hector is a skulking monster with a shaved head and gold hoop earrings. His arms are thick. His dark eyes reflect no light. He projects KILLER which is all we'll need for this job. Booster runs into the store to show what he can do. I watch him circle a rack of ladies' underwear and come back to us. He has a big, dumb smile on his face. I hadn't seen his hands move, but a flash of pink silk peeks out of the front pocket of his khaki Dickies. I'm glad this kid is good at something.

As I predicted, there aren't many customers in the store. One woman squeezes her swollen feet into a pair of beige high-heeled shoes. A skinny blonde pushes a basket of chic black evening wear. I mark five employees busy in stations around the store. We split up.

I carry three suits into the dressing room and layer one on top of the other under my original clothes. The dressing room clerk is preoccupied with closing his section—re-hanging discarded jackets.

"You gained weight, Maestro."

Arturo's wearing a white linen suit. His old clothes are piled on the floor of the dressing room. He adjusts the collar in front of the full-length mirror. Cecil found a dark 3-button suit from a tailor out of Chicago with a $1,500 tag dangling from the sleeve.

"Whichever way this thing goes down, you'll look sharp in front of the judge in court. Clinton had that suit when he came to speak at our school this year."

"What was he doing there?"

"Signing some education bill. I didn't get a chance to tell him to stop bombing poor people with cruise missiles. That school preached democracy, but only the politburo met with him in the library before the speech. Mr. Stone shook his hand. Fucker arrived in a helicopter."

I keep one eye, my left, on the employee closest to us—she's busy folding shirts. She doesn't seem like the type to risk confrontation. I find an overcoat in the men's section and a rack of ties that complement the suits. Despite the cool, still air, I'm sweating. The manager shuffles toward the exit, but doesn't acknowledge me, busy counting receipts from a closed register. Dandruff, like a fresh snowfall, covers the shoulder pads of her dark blue polyester jacket. Her face looks like an old brown lunch sack carried to school and back. I waddle through the front doors and expect the alarm.

"We stole everything that wasn't nailed down, Carnal, you know."

"Next time, bring a pry bar."

Juan pulls a dozen panties out of his pockets, pitching them into Cecil's truck. He presses one pair to his nose.

"You ain't supposed to sniff new pants, Joto."

"Shut up, man. They'll never smell like this again."

"Not after you're done wearing them"

Arturo punches Juan's upper arm.

"Let's go for another round."

His eyes are lit up like atomic fireballs—he wants to impress his cousin. A ruinous bravado and surrender to circumstances drive him toward a vexatious end. Wanting the cousin's approval, he stares into a take-it-or-leave-it face. Any meaning in the black, blank eyes remains open to interpretation.

"It's your call, Maestro. This is your gang."

"There's no boss here. We signed on as equals."

Cecil flicks an unfinished cigarette to the pavement. We go back in and pull off another round and a third until the truck bed can't hold any more clothes.

I hadn't seen the Security Chief; he usually skips his lunch hour, but sometimes groped or interrogated one of the clerks in the back room. Seeing him follow Arturo out of the store sets rage on boil in my brain bucket. Arturo and Booster went in to steal a fixture to hang all the new clothes on. Cecil told them he had some rope and could tie it on top of the camper shell. The Security Chief must think he can handle a couple kids on his own. Arturo's cousin Hector retains the tabula rasa stare, reads violence in my face and writes it into his short-term action list. His fists close.

"Excuse me…"

The Security Chief taps Arturo on the shoulder. Cecil steps from a shadow and cracks the fink on the side of the head with a mannequin arm. UGGGH. He staggers and spits gouts of blood and the occasional piece of broken tooth. The fiberglass arm splinters. Cecil jams the remaining shard between the bars of his rib cage and drops the Security Chief to his knees. I hadn't expected murder—I'd called myself a pacifist—but all the anxiety of my recent life swells to burst in my skull and seeing the rat-fink-fuck fall sends a howling ardor for revenge echoing out of the reptile brain—I step with a quickness and drive a Cross pen into his ear. The fancy pen was a gift from the school to teachers who were "moving on" (to pursue careers in poetry one imagines.)

The Security Chief twitches and shits his pants as Booster kicks him in the ass—a dark squirt of diarrhea spritzes Arturo's white linen mambo suit, which prompts Arturo to throw a cack-handed fist at Booster and catch him by the hair. Three rabbit punches pummel his kidney like a speed bag before I can yell in my rusty teacher voice.

"This fight is over."

Arturo freezes with his left hand gripped around Juan's hair and his right fist cocked.

"You messed up my hair, Homes; you ripped my shirt."

"We stole a hundred shirts, pendejo shit kicker, but only one white suit."

"Booster got himself a new nickname."

"Fits your country dumb ass, Shitkicker."

Arturo undoes the buttons and flings the jacket to the asphalt. We each kick the Security Chief one time for luck.

"Juan, go into the store and boost a white jacket in Arturo's size."

"Oh, man."

"Do it, Shitkicker."

"No problem, Hector."

Arturo smiles. Cecil wipes blood from the corner of his lip. Juan moves into the store like a ghost. The store will open tomorrow at 10am.

Unemployment

Free is not always so. Some things are cheaper than free. Other opportunities turn out to be expensive wastes of time. "Time is money" means nothing to a man without a job.

Next time some motherfucker asks you for the time, boogaloo and dance away, time ain't real no how.

Mr. Stone stepped outside of time. He moved on a different plane and his ability to switch between tasks so fluidly might be described as the true ability of winners in this scheme. He would be a master criminal, instead of a petty crook like me.

Bobby Dylan famously said, "When you got nothing, you got nothing to lose." But I say, when you got nothing to lose, everybody best stay the fuck out of the way. Every two weeks an unemployment check comes by post from the state, costing me little more than a stamp and a signature.

"Did you call the unemployment office?"

A week later, she asks again.

"The dole requires too much paperwork. An interview, hassle, deadlines."

I don't tell her I've rejected the concept of time along with the concept of work. I rest on a bank statement that shows enough money to lay off several more months.

"Please apply now. Listen. This is serious. Helen said after seven days off the job, the government thinks you don't want it."

"Well, I don't."

"You'd throw away six-thousand dollars?"

"Uhhh… Yup. The afternoon is open. Let's make love. Make life the book of love—a dime store pulp about drinking and fucking and fooling around."

"I can't have sex with a man who doesn't satisfy my needs."

"I'll rub you; I'll go down—whatever turns you on. *Going down south, going down south…*"

"That's all you think about."

"We haven't had sex in months. If I had sex, I wouldn't have to think about it. We'll get by. If that's what you're worried about."

"I'm not worried about getting by; I need some things. Poverty is not sexy, Dan."

"I don't know this, Dan. Entropy takes care of itself."

I realize, as I say all this, that random philosophical statements haven't been sexy since Camus died in a car crash. I pick up my shoes and shirt from the floor and put them in the closet and hamper, respectively.

"The reason we stopped having sex was because you haven't been able to get it up since you turned thirty."

Alaska knows how to castrate a guy in an argument.

"I was under stress; the job was killing me. Stress is the murderer of human potential. Teaching cuts a dick off."

I can't say why I've started cleaning the house. I toss a jacket into Caledonia's room. I wash the dishes, sweep the floor, wipe the pubic hairs off the toilet. The cat has been sleeping on the toilet again—blood-fat fleas left black and red spots on the porcelain. I wipe those off too.

"Jim-mee, think about your family, I'm not saying get a job, not yet, just apply for unemployment."

"Okay."

I heave out a vexed sigh. I open the phone book and fish a pen from under the rocking chair cushion.

"There's no listing under unemployment."

"Are you sure?"

We search the government pages, the white, yellow and other pages. About twenty minutes later, I discover that I'm going about this all wrong. I have it wrong from the philosophy on down to the practical application.

"Oh! I was supposed to search for Em-ployment. The Employment Development Department."

I dial the number and somebody puts me on hold. A bureaucrat comes on and tells me I missed the deadline to apply since the seven-day grace period has lapsed. So, if I want to collect, I'll need to write a letter of explanation.

When Cecil comes by the apartment around 11am, he finds me on the couch, in boxer shorts, drinking Bohemia from a brown bottle.

Employment

Eventually, I convince myself to leave the house. It's scary out here with people, fast-moving cars, trees close to power lines and all this sun. Speed kills. What if I get skin cancer? I ride my bicycle up Juniper Street and down Fifth Avenue to visit Rafe at the bookstore.

I pedal through the front door into the shop.

"The wild one."

Dismounting, I prop the bike up with the kickstand.

"Dig it, Jimmy, want a beer?"

I note three empties on the counter. A Bessie Smith 78 turns on the stereo.

"Oh. Wow, thanks, Rafe."

But instead of turning the volume up, he turns it down low so we can hear each other. A few customers browse the shelves. The book I wrote about teaching sits on one of them with Stewart Home's *No Pity*, Hemmingson's *Crack Hotel* and a coffee table book called *Sabotage in the American Workplace*. To my surprise, the young mod I'd seen dismount her scooter at Ground Zero lifts my book off the shelf.

"This any good?"

Her body's like a Modigliani—elongated neck, elegant hands, supple legs, lithesome torso. Her hair has grown out and her determined lips are coated with black lipstick. Born another kind of animal, she'd be a swan of Mallarmé.

"It's one of the great literary achievements of the century. A book that changes lives and shakes souls to the core of their being. Its passion calls to mind Marquez, its prose Fitzgerald, its honesty is unimpeachable and its integrity—legion."

She sets it on the shelf and picks up another book. She picks up *Lady Chatterley's Lover*, *Tropic of Cancer*, *City of Night*, *Our Lady of Flowers*… reading the back copy of each before setting each neatly into its place on the shelf.

After she leaves, Rafe adjusts a pair of green spectacles on his nose and compliments my sales job.

"No, no. She saw through me. I believed what I was saying, but she didn't."

"You can't sell books. You have to learn the customer in the first ten seconds, charm the mind and haply touch the heart, matching up her desire with the right book."

Rafer Youngman's girlfriend, Penny Le Guin, shouts out of the apartment at the back of the store.

"Jimmy, do you want to stay for dinner?"

"Thanks, Penny, what are we having?"

"Vegan lasagna with cashew ricotta."

"How'd you like a job, Mr. Jazz?"

The shop walls are covered with modern art. The shelves are jammed with good books.

"There are certain things I won't do for money. I'm not supposed to kill anyone or rob graves. Alaska laid down the law."

"We need someone part-time."

"Bookseller sounds like a sweet job. I love the smell of old books."

"Bibliosmia."

"Bibliosmia. You learn new things every day in a bookstore. I'd love to work here."

There's a feeling, when you are alone in a used bookstore, like walking through a famous cemetery. There's Kafka's grave and Tolstoy's. Bukowski is buried next to John Fante. Rimbaud lies over there with Verlaine. You look at the rows of graves and ask why there aren't more women. Literature must be some kind of war. In a small section near the potter's field, you find an ossuary with Kate Chopin and Jane Bowels, Dickinson, Hurston, Plath, Sexton, Stein, Nin, Duras, De Beauvoir, Lispecter, Arendt...

I went from $21/hour standard teacher pay with medical benefits to $4.75/hr. under-the-table clerk job. The benefit package here includes alcohol, hard bop played at full volume and an endless cavalcade of intelligent and freaky visitors. Some appear only to ask permission to use the bathroom. A similarity shared with teaching.

"There's no bathroom, use the one in the coffee shop, but don't buy coffee there 'cause the owner's a dick."

My first day on the job, this young, punk rock girl wearing a plastic mini-skirt, combat boots, black nail polish and a tight black tee with the blue circle insignia of The Germs walks into the store.

"Can you break a hundred?"

This is the twelve-year-old Lolita from the novel and not the sixteen-year-old actress from the film. Immediately suspicious, I throw her a weary sidelong glance from behind the counter. One of her friends picks up *Infinite Jest* and thumb-flicks the pages to feel its heft.

"Who gave you this Ben Franklin?"

I hold the bill to my nose. It smells like a cotton t-shirt out of the dryer. Like middle-class comfort.

"My mom gave it to me."

She smacks a piece of gum.

"Does your mom own a printing press? This looks counterfeit, spurious, ersatz, phony."

I hold the bill to the light, ball the paper and toss it into the trash can. She's not sure what to do. Her cool is breaking down. She reaches into the trash and fishes out the crumpled bill.

"I'm sorry. We'll come back later."

Her clique follows her out.

About ten minutes later, a couple of whacked out guys gnash their teeth on speed and jump into the store.

"Whoa, Kemo, dig the tat art."

He might mean the Picabia print or Lichtenstein's *Modern Art*. Kemo walks up to a large Robert Motherwell.

"Yeah, yeah, cool, cool."

His arms are sleeved with faded prison tattoos.

"Whoa, check this out."

Kemo and his buddy gape at a book of Charles Gatewood photographs. They flip from the classic picture of a four-hundred-pound nude to the silver body swami who holds a flame to his testicles in some New York disco.

"Sup, buddy."

"Sup."

Kemo has moved on to other oddities.

"I used to own my own tattoo shop."

"A pocket knife and a jar of India ink don't count."

"Funny guy. Whoa. Is that copy of *Under the Volcano* a First Edition?"

"It might be."

"Fuckin A."

"He had his own tattoo shop. Fuckin blew it though."

The friend shows me a half-finished eagle on his arm—a shiny object catches his eye and in ten rapid steps he crosses the store. He picks up a postcard, puts it down. His hands look dirty, like he lives on the street or fixes cars.

"Fuckin Johnny Law."

Kemo mumbles the word, "Hep-c." His eye catches something down the block.

"Whoa, check this out."

His partner has to sprint out the door to catch up.

About an hour later, the teenybopper punks return. Somebody broke the hundred.

"What should I buy?"

"What do you like?"

"Gritty, dark or post-apocalyptic prose."

"Have you read Burroughs?"

"Ya, I read *Naked Lunch, Junkie, Exterminator, Wild Boys*. I couldn't get into *The Nova Trilogy*."

"Come on, Jenny, let's go to the mall."

They split without spending money and I question my prowess as a bookseller.

"What's up, Jimmy Jazz?"

"Hey, man, waz up?"

"Gee, I didn't know you worked here."

"Need a particular book?"

"Ya, got any Kathy Acker?"

"There's an advanced reader copy of *Pussy, King of the Pirates*."

"Cool."

"It's five bucks."

He pulls out his wallet. I can't remember the cat's name. I either met him at an SF McBean art show or at a poetry reading. He seems too old to have been one of my students. I open a beer. My fourth. Thee Milkshakes come on the stereo.

Red monkey, whaa whaa whaa…

"Can you put it on hold for me? I'm tapped."

Hours go by without any customers. I read *Church Of The Sub-Genius,* which reinforces my lethargy. Their main tenant seems to be the reclamation of "slack," which we are born with but has been stolen by a conspiracy to indoctrinate an ethic of work akin to forced labor. Time-money justice was a lie. Civilized people punch a time clock. Consumers buy things. The time clock at Hard-Boiled Books measures empties instead of hours.

"I work the 8-bottle day."

I put my feet on the counter and listen to the Last Poets.

On the subway. I dug a man, digging me…

A guy walks in and pretends to browse the postcards.

"Is that the Last Poets?"

"Yeah."

I sip the beer and a cool wave of bliss rolls over me.

"Shoot, I owned one of their albums in the 70s. Those niggas were bad."

He looks around for some memory he left behind. Doesn't see the modern art or the books. He examines the walls, the architecture. He's on a slow drug, some anti-coffee. Sports a natural afro from the 70s and clothes that ducked out and ducked back into style.

"Fifteen years ago, you couldn't walk into this place. Chalkie's Pool Hall. Crazy fuckin dangerous place."

"You live around here?"

"I lived here from 74 to 79 with my old lady. The place has changed. Damn. Is this some kinda library?"

"*The library, the library.*"

"What's the name of that CD?"

I write *Last Poets, Last Poets* and add the equally great *Right On!* on a slip of paper.

"My friend Lulu picked it up at that record store off Midway."

"Those cats should get back together—name recognition in the community."

"You want a beer?"

"No thanks, brother. Never touch the stuff."

I retract the bottle and slide it across the counter.

The neighborhood has changed. Fancy restaurants with long-legged hostesses on the sidewalk lure high rollers. An epidemic of chain stores spreads out from the mall like spilled milk. Immaculately dressed motherfuckers gorge themselves on $200 meals and purge to stay thin like they live in a Roman orgy. A man on the street will point you to a parking space for the two dollars he needs for a bottle of undistilled wine. He'll watch your ride while you're in the restaurant—"So no one fucks with it."

The phone RINGS.

"Hard-Boiled Books."

A guy on the line says, "Sorry, I was looking for something over easy" and hangs up.

About an hour passes before this creepy dude walks in wearing a fine suit and mirrored glasses. He might be FBI. Might want to know which books certain readers read. Instead of asking who reads *The Satanic Verses* or *American Psycho*, he tells me he's a mortician. I suspected as much the second I shook his clammy, cold hand. He's got a pale pink piggy body, like a mouse dangled over an albino snake and smells of Old Spice and embalming fluid. He gels his hair back slick. He says he lives in an SRO down the block—a "charmer" with no windows.

"I'm going to Whiskey Priest for a Sacramental Wine Spritzer; is Rafe around?"

"Nah, he's not here."

Near closing, Rafe comes in with his dog. After hanging a drab brown fedora on the hat stand by the door, he walks into the back without a word. I take a knee and the dog licks my face. I rub him around the ears.

"Jimmy, any sales?"

"No ma'am, all quiet."

"Cookie?"

A small business may not be able to offer medical insurance, but they can bake cookies.

"Thank you, mmmm. I ruv cookies."

I stuff the whole cookie into my mouth and grab another before she shuts the lid.

"Um, Jimmy, we have to let you go."

"What? Why? I just started. I like this job."

I reach for a swig of beer, and at full tilt, see the bottle is empty.

"The landlord tripled the rent and business is slow. People aren't reading."

"Fifteen years ago, you couldn't even walk in this place."

I hear Rafe's voice.

"Chalkie's. Crazy fucking dangerous place."

I Heard a Word, Suicide

Home. Freezer. Bottle. Cold hands. I'd like to say the first shot rains down my gullet and warms from the inside, but it's all cold. Since my dismissal from Hard-Boiled Books, the plan has been revised to hit the local bar as often as possible. There's a dive on First and Juniper called The Bored Room which sells schooners of Miller High Life for a buck. A reasonable price. Caledonia is spending the night at a friend's house. Spending the night is the thing to do. Oh, how I remember those nights with friends. We would cavort into the wee small hours, from the pillow fights of youth to the pillow talk of later teen years. It will be a few years before Cali falls asleep in the back seat of a Ford Pinto or lays a blanket on a baseball diamond under the stars. As I pour another shot, I hear a strange noise.

Our cat's asleep on the clean linen. Alaska is in the shower. I put my ear to the bathroom door. I can hear the water fall and the loofah brush against her skin. I'd like to jump in with her, touch a nipple and drink at her fountain. I open the door—her blurred form stands behind the fogged glass shower door. She's so damn sexy; the blood courses through her veins. I hear the noise again behind me. A three-syllable MOAN. Down the hall, out the front door, I strain to listen, cross the bridge that leads to our apartment and step onto the neighbor's back porch. The noise is louder out here—a demented SCREECH—the drunk and unintelligible cry of a dying animal.

The sound emanates from Donny's open bathroom window. I'm afraid to look. Donny's a strappy little guy. A sailboat owner.

He makes toast in a high-volume breakfast restaurant. Denny's. Donny from Denny's. I got this information from one conversation on this same patio over a couple of beers. He has a boyfriend who sits at dull ease in solace on the porch, sips coffee and watches the Navy ships float to sea.

About this same time, my other neighbor, Indigo, peeps her head out the door.

"Jimmy, what's that noise?"

"Moo-ahh-deagggh."

We focus our attention on the window: glass, screen, black frame.

"Should I look?"

"I don't know. We don't know Donny well enough to get into his business."

I tiptoe to the window and put my best spy skills into action.

"What? What is it?"

"He's lying on the floor in his briefs… White BVDs. His boyfriend has him chained to the toilet."

The neighbors' love games are none of our business.

"Hey, do you want to go to The Bored Room with Alaska and I?"

"Sure, sweetie, we'd love to. Bart will be home soon."

You can tell that your neighbors are big drinkers when their bins clink as they drag them to the curb on trash day. Meanwhile, Donny bleats more ominous groans. His screech waxes coherent and falls back into "Moo-ahh-deagggh. Moo-ahh-deagggh." The sunset explodes over the harbor in a pink and purple sky show. The buildings light up downtown. It's a beautiful evening.

When Bart gets home, we decide to investigate. The lights never came on in the apartment, so Donny must be home alone.

"All right, I got a new theory. He's drunk. He's in the bathroom puking his guts."

Bart peeks in at the edge of the window.

"Donny's still face-down on the tile. He's in the luminiferous ether, man. Not on this earth."

Donny has a tiny body. I never realized how small he was. His thighs are as thick as Bart's upper arm. The bright white BVDs illuminate Donny's petite derriere.

"It's too dark."

"I don't think he's handcuffed."

Bart goes into his house and retrieves a flashlight. We look through the kitchen window first. Clean dishes on the counter, orange prescription bottles, vitamins, a toaster, two empty six-packs, salt, pepper, napkins.

"Moo-ahh-deagggh. Moo-ahh-deagggh."

"He's drunk."

Alaska comes out of the apartment to join us. She's all made up for a night on the town.

"Ree-ow kitty, revv-revv race car."

"We should call 911. He's in trouble."

"We should hold off our trip to the bar."

Bart produces four brown bottles from behind his back. We engage in conversational chitchat and decipher the moan.

"He's saying Michael."

"Moo-ahh-deagggh."

"Is that his boyfriend?"

"I think so."

"I got fired today."

"Again?"

"Moo-ahh-deagggh."

"We should talk to him."

About an hour has passed since Indigo and I heard the first groan. Bart walks up to the window. The rest of us remain near the patio furniture and cuddle our second beers. If I'm lucky, the accumulation of brown glass will continue to measure time.

"Donny, you okay?"

"Moo-ahh-deagggh."

The sun has set. There's no moon. Bart shines the flashlight into the bathroom window.

"He's out of it."

"Yerr-ee, yer-eee, moo-ahh-deagggh."

I walk to the kitchen door.

"Should we put a blanket over him?"

"Yes, Indigo, good idea."

 "He's small, we can put him in the bed."

"Will he thank us or get pissed?"

"I'd be embarrassed."

"Maybe we should go to the bar."

At this moment, Max and Cleyre Neuehaas appear.

"Hey, Max, over here."

Another "Moo-ahh-deagggh" startles Cleyre; Max looks in the bathroom window.

"What's wrong with that guy?"

"We don't know."

"Would you like to join us for drinks?"

"Thanks, Cleyre. We're going to hang here and see what happens. If this guy dies, do you want any furniture?"

"No thanks, man. We're going to the bar."

I pass through the kitchen door first while Bart points his flashlight beam. A couple of cat burglars. Bart finds the light switch in the same spot as his apartment but reversed. We survey the kitchen again—empty six-packs, prescription bottles show Prozac, Paxil and Lithium. In the living room, Bart switches on the light and we see an empty bottle of sleeping pills on the table next to a note:

> I couldn't stand the pain. Sorry,
> you had to find me. Please call
> my sisters.

"Call 911."

There's another empty pill bottle on the floor. Indigo and Alaska sweep into the apartment. Indigo gets on the phone. Bart and I barge through the bedroom toward the bathroom, toward Donny's inert body, but blood and broken glass cover the floor.

"He fell against the mirror."

"I knew we should call 911."

"Fuck. He rolled around in the glass.

"Moo-ahh-deagggh."

"Fuck."

Bart opens the bathroom door. CLUNK.

"His head's up against the door."

With some effort, we inch open the door. Donny's cries come clearer and more rapidly.

"Jerry. Jerry. Mayday. Mayday. Mayday."

"Don't touch him; he's all bloody."

"Ya, the paramedics have gloves."

We seize the opportunity to search the apartment. All four of us hold the note in our hands and read the text ourselves. We rifle his dresser for clues. There's a lot of spare change, a clean razor. A Denny's name tag says "Donny." I pocket a dollar in quarters.

"Maybe he has AIDS."

"Maybe his boyfriend dumped him."

"Maybe he's clinically depressed."

"That's for sure, look at these drugs."

A stack of photos shows him with his boyfriend at the dock, ready to set sail. I flip through his address book. Nothing. He wrote a poem on one of the pages—a single line, in blank verse, remains with most of the page torn away. Indigo finds his sister's phone number. She's got a bag from the kitchen and has already packed a set of clean clothes for him. She does practical things. Alaska hides our empty beer bottles.

"If 911 was Dominoes, we'd be eating a free pizza by now."

Everyone except Donny laughs. He screams, "Jerry, Jerry…
mayday, mayday."

San Felipe

"Jesus fucking Xist."

My bowels seize and a vicious cramp constricts my large intestine while an electric shock rocks the small one. I dash into the Trattoria Pesto, on 5th Avenue, with cold, shivering crazy guts ready to shoot. My stomach opens its yap like a lion—GRRRR—and turns the contents to liquid like a gas-powered butter churn. I scurry past the long-legged hostess at the door straight to the men's room. Swollen lips augmented to improve her pout. The only stall is occupied. No time, so kick the door—one Doc Marten boot against a flimsy hasp. The door SMASHES against the wall and springs back. A metal hinge ricochets to the floor TINK TINK TINK and I grab the guy on the pot by the collar. Pants around my ankles (he must think I'm here to fuck him) and I heave the poor bastard. His skull RAPS the opposite wall and he folds like an armadillo on the dirty men's room tile, clutching at his trousers.

I swing my ass over the bowl and let loose—farting, spraying shit. Earl Scheib should hire my ass to paint cars. The guy scrambles to his feet and runs for the door. He'd rather go around with a dirty butthole, than ask, "What the fuck?" and risk getting his head kicked in. He didn't even wash his hands.

Not what I ate and drank in Mexico but how much. My angry stomach served an eviction notice to the inmates of my innards.

San Felipe is on the Sea of Cortez, about six hours down a two-way desert highway. You head east on I-8, then due south through El Centro and cross the border at Calexico and Mexicali. Altars line the road—crosses, candles, flowers, photographs and toys—for the dead. A 130-mile-long cemetery. A lot of people died out here. In every crash a child ceases to exist. The sadness is heavy. Some headed home, others, like us, hoped to escape their routine. Desperate to leave their lives behind, they left their lives on the road. This focuses my attention on the two-lane highway, our speed and the oncoming traffic.

When Helga Kropotkin suggested the trip, it seemed like an inspired vision. Alaska and I were apprehensive about traveling with Helga, after what happened last time, but since we both needed a vacation. We ran into Mandy at Trader Joe's before we left and she decided to come with us, so we stopped at her place to pack a bag.

As we pull into a motel lot, I recall how Helga hid in the trunk of the car to save seven dollars at the Motor Court in Lawrence, Kansas on our road trip across the Western US. We used the windfall to visit the Museum of 500 Dog Figurines that Triple A's TripTik pointed us to. We missed the Museum of Custer's Stuffed Horse and The Garden of Eden, where some Civil-War-era kook created life-size cement statues from the Old Testament of the Hebrews and strange figures from the New Testament of his imagination. They say the museum displays his body in a glass sarcophagus, but poor timing saw us drive past the exit after nightfall. America isn't known to love its kooks or their wild imaginations while they're alive, but are more than happy to put any part of our history we can't deal with in a museum and charge a buck to walk through it.

I expect the proprietress at the motel in San Felipe to look at me funny when I ask for a room for three gorgeous women, but she doesn't blink. She's seen it all.

"We don't get many visitors in the summer."

"¿Porque?"

Helga talks to her in Spanish and from what I can comprehend, San Felipe is a popular Spring Break destination and November is a good time to visit, but only ignorant gringos would come here midsummer—it's well over 100° outside.

A pittance of cool air spits from the air conditioner. I'm exhausted from the long drive and gather enough energy to strip off my clothes and lay naked on the bed.

As soon as I close my eyes, Alaska puts her left hand on my cock and shoves it into her mouth. Mandy dances with debauched intent. Her breasts exposed, dark, nipples like chocolate kisses. Helga shakes her naked hips like a professional stripper on the other bed. She's opened a bottle of tequila and already laughs way too loud. That's the trouble with hotel rooms. The people next door always have more fun than you. She hops from bed to bed and this vacation is off to a fantastic start. It gets better as she straddles my face and wriggles her steaming vagina onto my mustache.

MMM. OOOOOO. MMMM. Soon the juice from her pussy covers my face and Alaska sucks my dick like it's the first time and the last, with passion undaunted by the unabated black sun. Her nipples change like the phases of the moon waxing bright and full and waning to a pink shriveled raisin. With Helga's ass wrapped around my face, I can't see or hear whatever machinations Alaska and Mandy slipped into. The distinct fume of asshole jams my senses. Mandy sucks my cock now instead of Alaska—a faster tempo with erratic rhythm and sharp teeth that scrape the shaft. Alaska's red nails dig into Helga's tits. The diamond engagement ring I gave her glistens in the light from a rent in the roller blind. Mandy slips fingers from her delicate hands into the other girls' cunts and we carry on in and out of each other until we fall into a jumble of twisted limbs for a collective nap.

When it's San Felipe and you have a hundred dollars in your pocket, everything is permitted, granted you can face the consequences. After a short siesta, we drink Tecate in the Sea of Cortez and all seems right with the world. A pack of wild dogs runs the beach. Silver streaks of flying fish shoot from the water. The sea temperature rivals the air for heat. It's too hot to move. We become part of the beach and huddle in the shade of a large umbrella which we carry into the sea. My chafed cock stings in the salty water—Alaska, Mandy and Helga splash like mermaids in the gentle surf. Helga laughs and a bunch of old men on the shore turn their attention, briefly, toward us.

Alaska swims up and wants to mount me again. She stretches one arm about my neck and reaches for my ball sac under the water with the other. Her legs float around my waist. Somehow my exhausted cock gets hard and the crazy sex ball starts all over in the Sea of Cortez.

"Pass the chips."

"Jazz, can you bring us another beer?"

"No problema, señoritas."

I hold up an empty bottle.

"Cuatro más por favor."

Helga dips a crisp tortilla chip into a bowl of guacamole. MMMM. Alaska looks beautiful and happy. We could alternate siesta and fiesta for the rest of our days.

"Hey, Honey, where's your ring?"

Her eyes shift to her finger, level off, and track over to Mandy. Conversation and movement at the table stop. There's a mural on the far wall that depicts an iridescent silver marlin's leap from the vermilion sea. Mandy's smile grows on her face until it signals embarrassment. I turn to Alaska.

"I left it in Mandy's ass."

"What?"

"Well… my finger slipped up…"

"Cuatro cervezas."

The waitress has pretty, full lips, big brown eyes and thick eyebrows that meet in the center like Frida Kahlo's. Underneath the table, Mandy digs into her bikini bottoms. A second later, she produces Alaska's ring.

"Tu diamante es muy precioso, señorita."

Our bloated bellies are packed with arroz, frijoles, tortillas, ceviche, tacos de pescado, camarones, chilaquiles, guacamole and cerveza. Endless bloody buckets of cerveza mas fría. I prefer Cerveza Bohemia but Tecate seems to have the town in a choke-hold. Almost every building has been painted with the red shield // black eagle standard of the company.

"The Tecate logo looks like Nazi propaganda."

"It's kinda scary."

"The rules here are less strict than in the Reich."

"A Weimar for the monied. Everything is permitted when you have money."

Ten dance clubs on the block that face the beach have been designed to entertain hordes of party-mad Americans. But in the too-hot off-season, we walk a deserted main street. Music BOOMS from ghostly discos. A local woman stops to sell us jewelry and Alaska buys a bead necklace for Caledonia. I go into a shop and study the fireworks. The girls all want to shoot bottle rockets, so we buy a quiver to launch on the beach. Helga and Mandy love to sip mescal, break things and shoot rockets—they live their lives in the moment like Roman candles. Inside the discos, we dance to the music in our own heads, determined to celebrate this day and this moment. One in flesh and spirit, we do not dance alone. As my old friend Shindig used to say, "Life is only once."

Las Vegas

Many people think that when you're on vacation different rules apply. I can't speak for firefighters or flight attendants (I can't even speak for teachers), so I'll speak as an artist, if poets are artists, and say vacation rules are the ones we go by all the time. We buck conventional morality and test its limits. If it works, go with it; if it doesn't, change it. I wrote a paper in college where I argued that suicide shouldn't be considered taboo. My English 101 professor didn't agree. My premise (there are too many people) was unproven and exposed an embarrassing lack of reading. She dismissed "My life, my choice" because a culture where suicide was permitted, would push certain people at the margins into an early death and leave the more privileged intact. She called my thinking "sophomoric," which was pretty good, since I was a freshman. My dad didn't like the essay either. He said life was good and that we were lucky. One shouldn't exhibit a zest for death. A writer needs harsh critics. Dad didn't like those melancholy poems where the hurt of being a teenager is too brash to bear. *The unfinished man and his pain.* Those years languished so far in the past, that if he looked back, the nostalgia was of a mettle that was never real. Any ennui or hard times set on a slow boil to evaporate. He remembered singing doo wop in the garage and meeting a Mormon at the drive-in who challenged people to debate religion. The Mormon was always barefoot and dad came away thinking Mormons didn't wear shoes. He said I should be grateful because I grew up with shoes and a roof over my head.

I've been having some trouble organizing my thoughts. I catch myself staring at the wall. At home, I cover my lapses in front of the tv on the couch next to Alaska or Caledonia. They never seem to notice that I'm not really watching. Reality cracks like an egg. The archeologist will find a thin white crack along my stripped and bleached skull. I got another odd job, which pays cash under the table, so now I am supposed to sell children's furniture. I've joined the merchant class, curious in that I despise capitalism and would give away the store.

"I can't sell things that don't sell themselves."

"Don't try too hard, but the clown suit is mandatory."

"A clown suit? Hmmm, can I keep it at my house?"

"Uh, I suppose… Jimmy."

"Call me, 'Poetry the Klown' with a K."

My makeup came together after careful study of a clown called Pogo, created by John Wayne Gacy, a famous serial killer. My new boss doesn't suspect that I may frighten the children with the sharpened corners of my smile. I slip into the red and white striped suit, glue pom-puffs on a stocking cap and paint some old white shoes I bought at the thrift store with red polka dots.

Alaska and I rent a car and drive across the desert to Las Vegas—we hit the strip like tourists. There's a pyramid and a sphinx—like we took a wrong turn at Albuquerque and wound up outside Cairo. A cartoon replica of NYC brings us back to the USA on a roller coaster. The guy in a cowboy hat behind us in a red convertible Lincoln Continental brings us to Vegas—

viva Las Vegas with neon lights flashing. In my rear-view mirror, a blonde wig bobs on the cowboy's lap. The cowboy wears dark glasses, hands at 10 and 2 on the wheel, stares straight ahead. The girl sucking his dick dresses like a prostitute. At the signal, he pulls up next to us and Alaska watches the girl's head rise and fall at an even tempo.

"Different sex laws here, eh?"

The work is like work anywhere. Small talk leads consumers to buy things. It's weird. I sell three thousand dollars worth of brightly colored furniture for my boss. An easy gig. She pays for meals and puts us up in a hotel. But her business needs help just one or two weekends per year and we'll probably blow our wages before we beat town.

Alaska and I walk down Fremont away from the strip and go into a local joint with a bunch of burned-out trailer park queens who play keno and drink Seagram & soda. Four men rest in leather armchairs on the nod in between games. One lady falls off a bar stool. Her ass hits the carpet and her wig slips off. She presses herself up like a contender off the canvas, adjusts the wig and mounts the stool for another round.

At the video poker machine, this Chuck Berry dude drops quarters into the slot with a blank stare—rocknroll sideburns jazzed up for Vegas. Smoke hangs in the casino air. Slot machines grunt and snort CHING CHING CHING. We don't see a single machine pay off as a hundred cigarettes burn down to the butts. One of those old characters whose throat caved in from cancer deals cards onto green felt. His name tag says Frankie. Frankie's eyes are an uncanny valley and the timbre of his voice a croak—like Clarence Henry, "*I'm a lonely frog, I ain't got a home.*' No one cares if he cares or has anyone to care for him. He's a cog in the money combine. The gamblers in this casino are locals; they aren't on vacation. Frankie Machine's livelihood depends on their addiction. Like my college roommate used to say, "A good parasite never kills its host."

We wander down the block and end up in front of a strip joint called The Donkey Show.

"What's the cover?"

"Five bucks each."

"My girl needs a job, okay if we check the place out?"

The door lady drags off a cigarette.

"She looks fine. Are those real tits? We like real tits. Check it out, Honeypot, can you put your leg behind your head like so?"

The old broad balances on her left leg and pulls her right behind her neck. She must be seventy years old. Alaska copies her move and both women balance like flamingos in front of the club.

"Those dance classes paid off."

"She can go in, but you gotta pay. No pimps. The girls here keep the money they earn. It's a union shop and we don't take no shit. My girls are treated right."

I hand her a five and we go inside. A red glow reflects off the body of a tall woman who dominates the mirrored stage with giant titties that curve at the nipples like the Matterhorn. Reminds me of Jumbo's Clown Room in Hollywood or the Pair O' Dice back home. I don't see a pinball machine.

In one corner, a young man negotiates the price of a lap dance. The dancer, a classic Rubenesque beauty, stepped impeccably from an oil painting of the 1620s. The young dude hands over a twenty-spot and the girl starts to gyrate, like one of those rides in front of the grocery store. Put in twenty dollars and the creature, which normally eats one quarter at a time, like a slot machine, goes rodeo bronco. She slides both tits from their holsters and squeezes a spray of milk into the guy's blissed face. She rubs the titties together like sticks friction up a fire. Pulling one to her mouth, she stamps a lipstick print on it while her loose hips circumnavigate the wet hot pussy hole under her silk panties. She's a great dancer but her song gives me a headache. Alaska and I are both surprised when she stuffs a tit into the customer's mouth.

"Different sex laws here."

"Milky bar."

A wiry young girl owns the stage now and rides the pole like a gymnast. If Olympic athletes still competed in the nude, she might shoot for gold. She puts both legs behind her head and spins around the pole like a tether ball.

On our way out, we pass the old lady at the door.

"Sorry Ma'am, she's not into being touched."

"You kids must hail from California. Nevada, Honeypot, runs under its own rules."

Alaska and I walk toward the hotel. Up ahead, three guys share a Colt .45 in the middle of the sidewalk. The first breaks off to greet us with a no teeth grin and nine o'clock shadow. Before he can speak, I look at the holes in my jeans and jab my hand out.

"Got any spare change?"

"Sorry, Buddy."

We walk on.

"Ha ha ha. That dude was so broke, he asked me for money."

Their rich laughter stays with us across the strip to the mall with the tourists and the light show. People all around us drink beer in the street—another privilege that is illegal back home. A guy who just walked off the golf links checks the time on a fancy watch. His cigar-flavored cologne reminds me of my grandfather. In the hotel lobby, I drop a quarter into a slot machine while we wait for the elevator. The wheels spin. A bar, a dollar sign, what's left of a cherry. Nothing.

Life's Stupid Details

I didn't come home from being drunk. I didn't call to say I was too drunk to come home. Alaska probably blames Cecil but it's not his fault.

He says, "Let's go to the bar and woo women, wooooo," to poke fun at jocks and fraternity brothers. He calls the local football fans "Dolts" and mocks spineless liberals and heartless conservatives; he hates yuppies and meatheads whose brazen shouts from safe places assault young girls, but enjoys a drink and isn't above meeting a woman in a bar. A complicated character, rife with contradiction. He talks like a misogynist and acts like a radical feminist.

My hypothesis is simple. If I can drink the entire bank account, hunger will force me to work a straight job and make everyone happy. A pint of beer costs $3 plus tip (give me a minute to do the math). Cecil thinks I should find a career and spend more time caring for my kid, which he never says out loud. We don't discuss personal issues, so I'm surprised when he tells me he wants to break up with Mitzy.

"She won't make out with me while I take a dump."

"Oh, sorry, man. I hate when chicks let their insecurities rule their passions."

He plays with Mitzy the way a dog plays with a rodent or lizard. The tail that breaks off will grow back. But when the neck snaps, the dog wonders why she won't get up. He still wants to play.

"She came over to pick up the last of her stuff and started to cry, the way some girls do, so I tried to fuck her, the way some guys do, in the ass, to show I could do her any time I wanted. I had her shirt off, at play with the boobies. She liked that. She got my pants down and sucked my schlong. I flipped her over on her tummy. Hiked up the skirt. Slid the panties down, left them dangling on one shoe. I had to shit, so I coaxed her into the bathroom. 'No, No, No,' she squealed and slammed the door on the way out. I sat on the toilet and knew I would always give her another chance."

"You're a dog."

"That means a lot from you. Let's go to The Live Wire."

I hold my hand over the phone and address my girlfriend, who knits a scarf on the couch.

"Hey, Alaska, can I go to Live Wire with Cecil?"

"You can drink beer and lay around hungover all day, but don't have time to consider my feelings? I didn't say get a job, D--… just send in the unemployment slips and give some time to your family."

"I'm a writer. I need to go to the bar to do research. I need you to give this project the same respect and consideration you would give a straight job."

"I give you everything. I'm the responsible parent. I drive Caledonia to tap; I shop, cook, clean, help Caledonia with her homework. I do everything and ask for nothing."

"Nothing?"

"Nothing."

"Could you rub me a little longer?"

OOOUGHH. She hates when I mock her voice and I expect a cup or a plate to fly but she hasn't got one in reach.

"You should have an orgasm and I shouldn't?"

"Ejaculation and orgasm ain't the same animal."

If he hasn't hung up, Cecil must think we're insane.

"I need more than a jerk off, I can do that for myself. There's a biological need to release testosterone and a psychological need to practice my technique. If you want the little guy to drive a long-haul truck across country, we gotta practice."

"Go jerk off."

"I already jerked off twice today."

I need to push one last button. Call it a sick need. I reach for the button; I pull my finger back. Reach; retract. It's like an elevator to the dentist's office. I don't want to go there.

"You don't even like sex."

"WHAT."

If I'm lucky, the sex strike will only last a week.

"You are so inconsiderate. You know that hurts my feelings."

We've had this same fight before.

"I can't fuck someone who doesn't treat me right. Now I won't want to for even longer. You knew that before you said it."

"I'll meet you at the bar."

I'm not sure how much time has passed. I'm wiped out, afloat in the hangover. I'm like that cloud on high above the hillside. Counting the flowers. I search for words behind each petal. I found *cacophony* there and *diaphanous*. I'm in a dream but if I move, the nightmare will rise from my gut reeking of flat stout. I puked some of the dead beer on Cecil's lawn. The alcohol passed over me like a freight train—CLACK, CLACK, CLACK—like I was a spiked-down tie between the rails.

We actually yelled "Woooo" at one point when our cerebral cortices had been suppressed, but not at a pretty girl. Cecil had the game of his life at the pinball machine. An epic high score.

Outside the bar, I sit on the curb. Cecil's inside, playing an extra ball with his pants around his ankles. I can hear (and even see) people walk out of the bar.

"Good night, Joe."

"Good night, Sam."

Everything you need to know, you learn from cartoons. I watch couples exit who went in single and singles exit who went in couples. I imagine all the complicated intercourse and study each newly formed pair to see how their bodies fit together.

"You're too tall… It won't work…Dane fucking a chihuahua… Better wear a condom with that one…"

Hands grope into pants through zipper holes. Hair follicles get stroked, birthmarks discovered, moles get mapped. Apartments like foreign countries or alien worlds. Come morning, "Where am I?" and "Who are you?"

I can see (so not gone) but can't move very fast—easy target for a lush roller. The speech center in my brain shuts down, probably for the best. I summon a force of will and climb into the back of Cecil's truck camper shell. At least it looks like Cecil's truck. I lay in the back and lean into the spin.

It was a crazy night at the bar. A happy hour with seven-dollar pitchers. I walked in, ordered a pitcher and asked for two glasses. Inch was playing on the jukebox. I sat at the bar. The bar tender pulled back on the trigger and a font of rich black stout flowed. Then this big Neanderthal walked over from the pool table at the back of the bar and tapped me on the shoulder.

"Can I see your ID?"

He stood even with the top of the door.

"Do you work here or are you trying to pick up on me?"

"I fucking work here."

I show him the ID.

"1966. It's ah 1996, ah, 96 minus 66 is ah 30."

He walks back over to the pool table.

"That fruity ass guy asked if I was hitting on him."

I carry the pitcher and pint glasses to the machine without spilling.

"Dumbass Neanderthal. I nearly left this high game in progress to whack the knuckle-dragger with a barstool."

Cecil shakes the machine to keep the ball in play. The thought of him stepping from the shadows with murder in his heart seems absurd.

Later, when he comes out of the bar, I mean to let him know I'm in the back of the truck, but still don't have speech control. I hear the driver's side door unlock. A serial killer in a horror movie sits on an ax in drag. I'm an urban myth, a solitary man in the shadows. A murderer lies in wait. A hobo grabs a handful of box car.

She moves along like a cannonball, like a star on its heavenly flight…

I ride all the way to his pad, bump and yaw left, and imagine sideral islands in the black-dark Wyoming sky framed through the reefer hole of a fifty-car train. He drives slowly and carefully, the way drunks drive. When we stop, I hear the cab door slam, but can't move. He goes into the house and greets the dogs.

"Daddy's home. RUFF RUFF RUFF."

I pull a tarp over me and sleep with the spare tire for a pillow. I can't say how much time passed, but need to puke and climb out of the truck. I feel dizzy and chuck onto the lawn. OOOAAAGGHH.

"You burned a circle in the grass with your puke, man."

I told him I was sorry but wasn't. It was the kind of perfect circle that doesn't exist in nature. An apple falls on Newton's head and Archimedes pukes out his guts and invents geometry. I grovel up onto the porch and wait until I hear footsteps to the bathroom. When the toilet flushes, I bang on the door.

"What are you doing here?"

"Sleeping on your couch."

I crash onto the sofa and one of his dogs licks my face. He probably told her to do that. His other dog puts his wet nose—snout to snout—a centimeter from mine, so in brief flashes of consciousness, I feel the dog's hot breath.

Sometime after the sun rises, Cecil says to the dog, "Kill the poet," which touches an emotional center in my brain. He might be the only one who really believes I'm a poet. And if I'm worth killing, I'm worth something.

A Rocknroll Poet, Wooooo

On the death day of Charles Bukowski, I wrote a few words on a bar napkin in his honor. I called the poem *74 Is Old Enough*. The bard of the barflies lived a good long life—he drank his liquor with fervor to the end without remorse or regret. In the poem, I contemplate my future as a senior citizen: drinking, fucking and/or jerking off to classical music: Mahler, Shostako-vich, Sibelius.

I'm sitting in another dive bar and drinking the black from a bright red plastic cup in a dark red vinyl booth with Cecil and Lulu Rivers. Cecil's been chain-smoking clove cigarettes and we've been flicking matches at each other. The jukebox plays The Stooges *Your Pretty Face Has Gone To Hell* and a heavy cloud of smoke hangs in the center of the room between the arc of the bar, the stage and the pool table, which has been pushed back against the wall to accommodate the loyal fanbase of The Seven Elevens. Steven Eleven, who plays guitar, slides into the booth next to Lulu.

He looks into her eyes as they speak. If their relationship is sexual, it doesn't show on his poker face. Her thoughts are hiero-glyphic—filmmakers think in images. He strikes me as polite and sincere like his music. Lulu says he likes gay leather cow-boy bondage movies, but doesn't let on how she knows this. As far as I know, he hasn't been in any of her films. I suppose film students and musical geniuses and amateur poets occupy every city of at least a million. In the bigger cities, they compete for places to play.

"Stevie, you should call Jimmy up on stage to do spoken word with the band."

Skeptical, he sips from his own red plastic cup. We've spoken a few times but never talked. I've seen his band play a dozen times and own one of their records. This does not embarrass me. Like, what if *Goodbye Ruby Tuesday* was on the stereo and Keith Richards knocked on your door to bum a cigarette? Steven has nicely trimmed brown hair and broad, square shoulders. He smells a little like Vietnamese food and dresses like a college student. He slides out of the booth and says he has to tune his guitar. Cecil and I order another red plastic cup of beer and one more before the band takes the stage.

The jukebox cuts off and the house lights dim. CLICK, CLICK, CLICK. Melvin Eleven, the drummer, cues a tremendous wall of volume that floods the room like storm surge in a hurricane. The sound wave washes away old pains and new worries and lavishes listeners in a bath of bliss. A long-haired dude in front of the stage wads a napkin and stuffs his ears—if I live to seventy-four, I'll be as deaf as Beethoven. The music, a mishmash of genres, combines old styles in trenchant ways—instrumental surf and sidewinder jazz and THUMPING punk rock bass set in klezmer time. I'm pretty drunk and stand to the side with Lulu and Cecil, who hocks up a loogie from the depths and spits its flesh on the floor. I ask the bartender for a pack of matches and a red plastic cup of water to slow down, come back to earth, wanting to sober up. But the alcohol's all over me like a hot young chick tearing at my clothes, fumbling with my belt buckle and I tear back at her like a sex starved lunatic. The bra-latch is one clever snap of the fingers away. So far away. Angora sweater flung carefree to the hardwood. Fuck the world. My head rocks to the driving music.

"Jimmy Jazz."

Was my name spoken through the columns that nestle the p.a.? Who the hell is Jimmy Jazz? I straighten my posture and raise my hand like I was called on in class.

"We're going to hear a poem from Jimmy Jazz."

Steven says my name into the microphone. Heaven Eleven, the saxophone player, gestures for me to hurry while Llewellyn Eleven, the trumpet player, extends a muted note into eternity. Cecil pushes my shoulder and meets equal resistance. He brandishes a matchbook, ready to flick a lit match at me. His Belushi-eyebrow seems to signify "there's nothing to lose" and that he intends to set me ablaze either way. I look to Lulu for help, but she's talking to someone at the back of the bar. Alaska stayed home with the kid. There's nobody here to stave off humiliation. My kid deserves more than a failed teacher for a father, her father should be a great poet and cool rock star—I'd love to draw inspiration from her, but it's the wrong brand and not what's required, so I let the thought die.

I step to the microphone. The band drives forward. How good music and bad reasons sound when one marches against an enemy. The bright stage lights eclipse the fans in front of the stage; I was one of them a few seconds before. The music runs over the hills like wild horses. Kevin Eleven, the bass player, bangs his shaved head and makes an angry face like he hates every note. The keyboard player bangs the keys like a percussion instrument. The packed dance floor precludes dancing. It's like the killing floor in a slaughterhouse. A crucifix in a deathhand. It never goes away. Never changes. It always stays the same. Consumers queue three-deep for the bar and five-deep for the pissoir. It's that time of night when more people are pissing than drinking. Cecil says, "Don't break the seal." Once you break the seal, you might as well camp in front of the urinal. A young girl dances on the billiard table—it's the mod with black lipstick; her bangled arms suspended above a shock of hair that hides her face.

There's no time to invent a stage persona. I'm terrified. I close my eyes and find that the alcohol has subdued my inhibitions. My arms stretch perpendicular to my torso and I balance the water cup on one palm. I'm a cliff diver and face the surf that surges between the rocks below. I focus on the red plastic cup. AHHHH. The music rises before a crescendo and I BAT the stupid cup at the crowd and anoint the long-haired dude in front of the monitor who, so busy stealing the set list, doesn't notice.

"Yeah-eah-eah ay. Okay mutherfuckers, how many people here have read a book?"

No hands go up. I'm an anticlimactic idiot, a poet who acts more like a teacher than a rock star.

"How many people have read a book by Charles Bukowski?"

Hands rise slowly around the room. Maybe they're afraid I'll give them a quiz.

"He died a few days ago. He died for your sins. He died so you could get drunk here tonight."

Red plastic cups rise in toast around the room.

"To all my friends."

"More people have read books by Charles Bukowski than have read books…"

The drummer hits a rim shot without a break in the beat. The music surges forward.

"I live a dainty life of healthy intake, fat free, sodium free, orrr-ganic, I don't smoke, I drink in moderation to temper the heart…If I'm not blind, think of the books I'll read…If I'm not deaf, think of the music I'll here…."

Time folds in on itself, the poem is over, the song ends—but I don't know what to do, so I step off stage back into the crowd. The band plays the next song and that's it. That's what it means to be a rock star—to dream your whole life, to listen late at night to KPRI when they play Soft Cell or Iron Maiden and think, "Wow, that's so cool and weird, wish I could do that." Fantasies get fulfilled. Perfect daydreams end like perfect days. Sonny and Cher played here in the 60s. I've seen GBH and DOA. Johnny Thunders got high and wailed on his Les Paul like a widow at a grave. Cliff Cunningham leaned on his peg leg and sang *Psycho Ward*. Keith Morris screamed at the crowd and so did Dez Cadena and Henry Rollins—all in different bands. We danced to The Pandoras wild set and stayed home the night GG Allin shoved a bottle up his ass on this stage.

The real history of rocknroll has been made here. GG Allin and Paula Pandora are dead. Sonny died on the ski slope and Johnny died from drugs. Cher became so famous that she never had to play this dump again.

Lulu chats up the youthful mod who danced so well on the pool table. The bar closes and everyone gets pushed outside onto the sidewalk. There's no limo waiting—I can't remember where we parked the car. A man sleeps on the sidewalk in front of the liquor store across the street. On the long walk home through the night, Cecil and I are still trying to light each other on fire, one flaming match at a time.

The Bums are at the Beach

Caledonia's legs pump as she races her school chum, Katrina Karadzic, to the soccer ball on the green at Mission Beach. Another perfect day fades. The coaster RUMBLES under the high-pitched squeal of a young girl. Time hates us with the sun perched on the high-dive, studying the sea.

"Jimmy. Jimmy, can we steal a moment for adult discussion?"

She wants to discuss the future, at least the near future, but my mind slips into the past.

"Jimmy, find a real job."

It's a fair statement that I mean to consider before answering. I sit around the house in my underwear and search for pareidolic images in the textured plaster walls. Images abound, but no art.

"I'm serious. Let's talk about this. Your unemployment checks are going to run out."

I breathe out carefully to avoid a sigh. A bum strikes dirty fingers against the gut strings of a guitar.

"Alaska… Alaska… babe… uh… I don't want to work."

I rub my hands together even though it isn't cold. Katrina reaches the ball; Caledonia kicks, dribbles, loses control when her shoelace unfurls, the ball caroms toward the boardwalk, a detour, she circles around… Katrina runs with her arms spread like a gull, mimicking the bird overhead. Caledonia lines up squarely: kicks. Her right shoe turns end over end in the air. The black and white checkered ball rolls on target to my feet.

"Goal."

Alaska folds her arms across her chest, shifts the weight from right leg to left. I pick up the ball and at dull THUD—it soars as with its own wings, bounces and rolls across the grass. The girls run to fetch it again. Kids are like dogs.

"Have you thought about what you want to do?"

"Not really… Don't you think more people should be here playing on the grass?"

"Not really."

When I was a kid, Mission Beach's Belmont Park was haunted by carnie pitches and the seedy smell of sugar and nicotine. My hippy uncle Rich and aunt Mimi used to bring me.

"Every game a winner; a winner in every game. Take a chance and win your gal a prize."

A sad patina of genuine joy stuck to everything like cotton candy. A dozen sailors mixed with boys and girls in line for caramel apples. Ferris wheel in the sky keep on turning. Fat pigeons choked on popcorn and hot peanuts. The air was filled with risk. The dying amusement park reeked of neglect like a tenement abandoned by an absentee landlord; it was doomed. The asphalt was littered with ticket stubs and smelled faintly of piss. The Wild Angels ruled the wall along the boardwalk; their Harleys lined up near Hamel's bike shop. A kid pukes out of The Spinner and heaved soda and hot dog mush at a garbage can, laughed some out his nostril. Husky biting flies hung over heaps of rotten garbage. The Funhouse threatened to swallow us whole. But where now the whip-crack of The Wild Mouse and the dizzy heights of The Hammerhead? Carted off, I suspect, to carnivals in Piqua, Rochester, Wilmot… What happened to the rock-n-bobsled that crushed our family together? ¿Donde esta el sideshow? The hideous laughter ricochets through the universe. The crab people live. A skywriter bi-plane scrawls the word COPPERTONE between us and the sun. What about the dime-toss where you could win a KISS, *Love Gun* mirror, Hang Ten ashtray or a troll with yellow hair?

RING the bell with a hammer. POP the balloon with a dart. Lasso the milk bottle. Toss a softball into a peach basket. Where are we gonna find a milk bottle and/or peach basket when the millennium hits?

The coaster RUMBLES under the high-pitched squeal of a young girl.

They outlawed horse diving off the pier, took the gymnast rings off the beach and before you know the long-chained swings get replaced by shorter chains.

My mother swam at The Plunge when it was a warm saltwater bathhouse in 52, where flapper's promenaded with their gents twenty years before. They razed the crumbly Spanish plaster building and erected a glass and steel greenhouse over the old pool. It's part of a fitness gym now. They took out the high dive and the low dive and put up a "No Diving" sign and liability waiver at the front desk. They bleached the old mildew smell and let the chlorinated fog of the 70s dissipate.

They built a mall around the Giant Dipper roller coaster—constructed in 1925 by a crew of men hired by John D. Spreckels; and burned in 76 by arsonists cooking food or keeping warm. The redevelopment team put in retail shops to pay the rent. Added a cruelly slow carousel for babies. The city cleaned up the park, sterilized it and rendered it deceptively safe. You can use the restroom now. But that rickety old wooden track will break your neck and your back. EEEEEEEEEE.

A better proportion of this city's million and a half people should come to the beach to watch the sun set every night.

A tourist tries to snap a photo of the ocean that doesn't have a bum lingering in the background. The coaster RUMBLES under the high-pitched squeal of a young girl. Two gulls peck a discarded potato until one flies with it out to sea. A host of sun-blackened winos gambol along the cement wall of the boardwalk and drink beer from 40s in paper sacks. A radio plays Zeppelin.

And she's buying the stairway…

"If you don't want to work, tell me what we're supposed to do for money. You know rent?"

I can taste the salt air on my lips.

"Things like that take care of themselves. They always work out."

Caledonia jogs up and holds the ball against her tummy.

"Daddy, mommy, can we play Monkey in the Middle?"

"Sounds fun. You're the monkey."

She tosses the ball in the air and jumps into the middle.

"Caledonia is a monkey, a monkey, monkey, monkey…"

I tease that we got her from the zoo, shaved her and taught her to speak. She plays along and acts infuriated. A repartee from one of our routines. I kick the ball to Alaska who kicks it past Caledonia to Katrina.

I hear the waves break on the sand and kick the ball to Caledonia.

"Now I'm the monkey. Ooo Ooo Ooo."

I scratch under my armpits and jump up and down. Turn a somersault on the grass.

The girls laugh.

At this point, this old orange-skinned rum-guzzler forsakes his place on the wall and approaches us. He walks without apprehension, like a man driven by an idea. Alaska wants me to take action. I expect him to ask for change or a cigarette.

"I used to play soccer when I was a kid in Rhode Island."

He remains two body-lengths away. A mother mountain lion stands between him and the cubs.

"So, you came from Rhode Island?"

"Lived in Hawaii too. I been all over."

The girls continue kicking the ball.

"My name's Pete."

Pete wears faded blue denim jeans and a dirty button-up shirt. The frayed cuffs on the jeans are wet like he's been walking the beach with his shoes off. His white tennis shoes don't fit right, probably a size too big.

"Can I play? Don't worry. If you want me to go, say the word."

He sweeps his hand toward the horizon. I guess he means he'll vanish, become invisible. Or return to the sea. Caledonia hops in the middle. Alaska kicks the ball to Katrina, but it glances off the side of her foot and rolls right to the bum's feet. A triangle becomes a square, doubles its size, by adding one point.

"My name's Pete. What's yours?"

He kicks the ball to me. Caledonia sidesteps and intercepts.

"I'm Jimmy."

"Caledonia."

"Katrina."

"I'm Marianne."

Alaska proffers a pseudonym. I forget that you can lie to strangers. You can invent identities and personalities. I wish I'd made up a name too.

I expect Caledonia to say, "You're not Marianne," but instead she points at the rum-guzzler and says, "You're in the middle."

Pete sets up and steadies his feet. We kick the ball past him. He moves, spins, swings a leg and falls on the grass. He's schnockered. He gets up. Caledonia kicks the ball to Katrina, back to Alaska, across to Caledonia. Over to me. He can't get the ball. We have him turning circles, dizzy, so that he falls at more frequent intervals.

"Okay girls, in soccer you have to use your head, think."

He taps a dirty finger on his skull. Caledonia kicks it past him. Cynical me thinking—look where it got me, I'm a wino. I live under the pier at the beach. Then I remember the time Alaska and I made love under that pier, the moonless night was so dark we couldn't see each other. Eventually, Pete gets the ball. He loses equilibrium as he kicks, falls again. Katrina's in the middle. We've extended our family. Uncle Pete smiles and reveals a broken tooth. He has a scab on his forehead. He smells of stale brew and fermented sweat. And kelp. He smells of dead kelp. When he kicks the ball to Caledonia, he does a soft baby kick so dainty, afraid he might hurt her. She puts a solid leg to it and rockets the ball past him. He jogs to chase it. Bums are like dogs, too.

The sun sets, a brilliant explosion of pink over the Pacific. There's some green in it, you see the blue, some purple. It's time to go. It's clear Pete wants to keep playing.

"Hey, Pete, we have to go now."

He steps close like he wants to shake my hand.

"I had a great time."

He puts his hand up for a high five and I clap my hand against his. He gets a five from the girls too. Caledonia smacks his hand hard SLAP. Katrina doesn't want to touch him, but he waits with his hand vertical until she slaps it. He approaches Marianne for the final five and includes a warm-fuzzy elbow squeeze.

"Thanks, mama. Thanks for letting me play."

Pete waves.

"I love you."

That was never a problem for his generation; it was in every song.

We pile into the car and Pete walks over the grassy knoll silhouetted against the ocean. He waves again. We all wave.

"Was that guy poor?"

"That guy was drunk."

"I smelled alcohol on his breath."

"I smelled drugs on his shoelaces."

Katrina utters the best line. After that, we rent a video and purchase a half-gallon of cookie-flavored ice cream.

Poets Are Klowns

"Alaska, should I wear the clown suit to the poetry reading?"

"What?"

I walk into the bedroom wearing the clown suit; Alaska shakes her head.

"Why not?"

"Because no one will take you seriously."

I adjust the fright wig in the full-length mirror.

"Poetry is too serious; that's why no one likes it."

"You plan to wear a clown suit and read those disgusting poems in public?"

"That's right."

"You are insane."

"Do you wanna do it?"

"Go away."

The bar, way out in suburban La Mesa, is smaller than a typical dive and narrow like a hallway. The poetry reading benefits a run for Congress by a friend of ours. She plans to spend no more than five hundred dollars on the campaign (if she had a hundred million, she wouldn't waste it on tv commercials). Our daughters are in the third grade together. When I arrive in the clown suit, she doesn't seem the least bit fazed.

"Right on."

The fact that she isn't surprised by anything I might do connects with the slim chance she has of being elected. During the Republican Presidential Convention, she walked 5th Avenue in a pig mask. You can't imagine Lyndon Johnson in a pig mask. Or Strom Thurmond. Many US senators look like they're wearing pig masks, but they aren't. So far, I'm the only performer on time. If I say, "See you at nine," I'll be there at eight-fifty-nine. I learned this from my dad and his dad, for whom punctuality was a cardinal virtue.

"Jimmy, those two women at the bar came to see you."

A conservatively dressed pair of ladies with severe lips perch on stools near the end of the bar. Each has a can of 7UP next to a glass full of bubbly clear liquid.

"They must be from the N.O.W. I'm supposed to do a gig for them next week to save Affirmative Action."

"That's cool."

"Yeah, I dunno. Affirmative Action is a lovely concept. Same pay for same work. A handicap for subpar schools in bad neighborhoods. Too bad you need to work to take advantage."

My friend the congresswoman has a tattoo on her biceps of the Westinghouse Woman, often confused with Rosie the Riveter. Again, a noble woman in every aspect, but famous for working. I don't see anyone's liberation bound with the right to work a meaningless job.

"I'm against work. Against crap you don't want to do but do—for money. You can't work over time. Overworked and underpaid is a cliché. Toil, serfdom, indentured servitude. Whichever way you parse it, work deeply entangles with slavery. These words are curses. A cubicle is a kind of prison. Automation is the key, robots. Valerie Solanas had the right idea. Except for the part where all the men are cut up into tiny little pieces and discarded… uh… Sorry, if I'm talking too much. I'm nervous and drank too much coffee. I drank a lot of coffee. I mean, we call somebody who tries to kill himself crazy. We say a girl who cuts herself has a compulsive disorder. Well, I say people who work are mentally ill. People literally work themselves to death. Not just a few consumers afflicted with carpal tunnel who try suicide, I mean heart attacks. Stress from work kills more people than any other affliction. Heart disease is number one. Gotthold Lessing said we should be 'lazy in everything except in loving and drinking, except in being lazy.' Could you include Zero Work in your platform?"

An aged hippie, bald on top with long hair in the back, has stepped up to talk with her. "Congratulations on your challenge to the system." Being a politician sounds too much like work for my taste. I sip the first compensatory pint of Celebration Ale—a poet paid in wine follows tradition—for we do not accept hard currency. I'm just another clown on a bar stool, but in full regalia. Alaska sits to my right and Cecil to my left. The last time we came to this bar, we got crazy out of our minds drunk. The bartender went into the back and Alaska poured herself a beer but pulled the fancy tap handle right off. Broke the fucking thing. "I've had eighteen straight whiskies, a record." She got angry and dashed out the door that leads to the street. By the time I got to the door she was gone. There aren't many people on the suburban streets after midnight. Cecil and I walked the streets, "Alaska. Alaska." Two hours later, we sobered enough to drive home. I was ready to call the hospitals, but she was asleep in our bed.

The bar grows more crowded as the night progresses. Each new patron sneers at the clown suit.

"What? A klown can't stop in for a beer after a hard day of yuks? Yuk yuk."

By the time I step onto the stage, I'm roaring drunk.

"All right motherfuckers, I am now your klown."

"Poetry."

The bar band who played this joint the night before stole the microphone, so I yell. I don't care. When I'm called, I jump up on the long thin bar itself and speak my first poem—about a boy in Caledonia's class abused by his parents. Half way through, two rednecks walk in. Bucky Sinister says in a poem of his own that the difference between hicks and rednecks is that hicks are merely religious, while rednecks are spiritual.

My plan of attack, to win their votes for my friend, involves the voters in the performance, as if taking part in the spectacle was less nauseating than being a spectator. Walk toward rather than away from conflict. I repeat the chorus louder and louder. "Jesse's mom beats him, Jesse's dad beats her…" I jump off the bar and pogo through the narrow space behind the row of barstools.

Jessie's mom beats him, Jesse's dad beats her.

I repeat the lines as I inch closer to the rednecks. I thrash and scream my mantra.

"This is not a poetry reading. This is not a poetry reading. This is a fucking tantrum."

I step right up to the tallest guy's face, so close I could strike a match on his jawbone and yell, "Jessie's mom beats him..." I lost cognizance of anything but the phrase. I can't see the bartender or the future congresswoman or my friend or my lover or the women from N.O.W. No one here but a little boy exploited by his parents. Beer sloshes out of mugs, bar stools teeter. I throw myself at the redneck's heeled cowboy boots and beat my head on the cement floor THUNK THUNK. Usually, when a poet pauses, the audience takes a cue to applaud. I hear scattered claps around the room, I guess it's over.

Alaska touches my back with her healing hand, a pang of comfort. Blood runs from an open wound. Cecil drags me out the back door.

"What were you doing?"

I could heave out all the free beer. I seethe and boil over with contempt for the human race. A thin red line of blood drips from a cut above my eye.

"Banging my head against the world."

The future congresswoman comes out onto the sidewalk with us. She pats me on the back. I'm bent with hands on my knees, ready to pass out.

"That was rad, Jimmy."

"Don't encourage him."

"He thinks he's Darby Crash."

"Or Iggy."

"Hanx."

My voice has crapped out for the first time since I quit teaching, which is what I get for using my vocal cords as a slingshot to slay passersby.

"You shouldn't scream like that."

Alaska hugs me and I'm not sure whether I'm misunderstood or understood too well.

The next performer runs into the bar in a loincloth, without a shirt, and carries two flaming tiki torches. He whips them around to capture our attention and sprints out the back door. The voters on the barstools set their pints on the long, thin bar and follow him out into the parking lot. He picks up a bucket of gasoline and sets it alight with one of the torches. He swings the bucket in a circle. The centrifugal force creates a nice optical effect with the fire until some of the flaming gasoline sloshes onto his hand. His teeth clamp together hard. Skin bubbles and POPS. The smell of burning human flesh excites madness in the hungry. You can see his mind calculating a next move. The flaming gasoline trick spirals out of control. He wants to move the bucket away from the crowd—but two quick steps see his knee buckle and the bucket whips loose from his grip and turns end over end through the air—tail arc like a comet—and SPLASHES onto the hood of a parked car. The burning gasoline ignites some dry bushes and the flames lick one layer of paint off the building, like a starved goat will lick the sole off a bare foot. The future congresswoman seizes control of the disaster and dumps a bucket of sand on the situation. The preordained chaos showed how calmly she works under pressure—smart where others panic. She saved the bar from burning down. But, of course, some rat fink called the police. Wherever you are, whatever you do, somebody will call the police. Cops will interrogate. Witnesses will give contradictory statements. The performance artist fled the scene, which left no one to arrest. The future congresswoman had been to jail many times, but never for a reason less substantial than the cause. A story appears in the local paper a few days later—more factoid than fact—but the publicity was not sufficient to help our friend, the congresswoman, carry the election.

Red Light District Opium Den Party

André was the first person we saw bathed in red light. A mixed drink in one hand, a cigar in the other. Everyone agrees that he's a beautiful boy, with his long black hair gathered in a ponytail; supple youth drips from his skin and his freshly charged Art Spirit sparks the air. He sports a paisley-lapel smoking jacket. The cigar, wet with his saliva, isn't lit, though most of it has been smoked.

"Jimmy Jazz, Alaska."

"Hey, André."

"I thought you weren't coming to this party because you had a job playing Santa at a group home?"

"He was supposed to play Santa, but he got fired."

"You can't hold on to a job."

"Yeahhhh, well, last year's Santa showed up. The guy had his own suit. You know."

"Sorry."

"That's okay, all that drooling and screaming gives me the creeps anyway."

"We saw your painting at the erotic art show…"

Alaska gets cut off when one of André's homosexual friends pulls him aside to meet a guy in leather chaps.

Campus Avenue has the best parties. "Red-light-district Opium den" means they changed the light bulbs for red ones. A triple birthday: Helga, Mandy, André. The cake has already been cut into, so if there was singing, we missed it. Devil's food with plain white icing and a raspberry center. Alaska and I cross the hardwood floor to the snack table and I stuff Seamus' homemade falafel into my mouth one after the other and dip each in a creamy tahini. Seamus rests on the chaise lounge, half asleep, with his brow furrowed by time and a glass of red wine balanced on his belly. Hypnotic music subtly intoxicates. Mandy flits to each clique, like Tinkerbell the party hostess, to see everyone has a drink.

Helga's clique monopolizes the couch in the corner. She's locked in conversation with Janet X, one of those local rockers who works at the record store. They laugh at private jokes. Janet complains about her husband, who doesn't like parties. Eddie, the new young boy, sits at Helga's feet. He's younger than the last one, but surprises you with moments of high Zen mysticism. He's wearing a costume, though it's not a costume party.

"What's your costume, Eddie, straight white male?"

"I'm a disgruntled white male serial killer."

He tucks a big plastic hatchet into his belt and under his ski vest.

"I'd be a cannibal too, but I'm food conscious and most people are too fatty."

Alaska and I switch to Oreo cookie insertion and stuff one after another into our mouths like we only eat at parties, free sample giveaways and art openings.

"Mmm."

I mix us both vodka/cranberry because there isn't any whisky or wine on the table.

Alaska starts her conversation engine with a couple of guys in another clique. She has the ability to talk to strangers, which I find incomprehensible, yet marvelous. They are obviously homosexuals. The obviously heterosexual clique stands in the opposite corner.

Some guy whose name I can't remember approaches.

"Do you want to smoke some pot?"

"No, thanks."

I prefer to sit alone in a folding chair and sip my cocktail. Shonenberg, Mandy's beau, and Mr. Folds, Mandy's housemate, sandwich a twenty-one-year-old girl between them. Shonenberg has her hand clenched in his and Mr. Folds massages her shoulders.

"Would you dally with us in sex, if we were the last men on earth?"

"Perhaps."

She toys with them—savors the attention. Her wide wan countenance and glossy brown eyes are acutely accented by the chartreuse and gold 50s lamp on the end table. She's wearing a chic leather coat. She pulled her black hair back and gathered it onto her head with a hairpin Mata Hari might steal a spy's life with.

"What if I was the last man awake at this party?"

As the party surges forward, we drink and drink and drink. The music keeps us swaying. Mr. Folds has an extensive collection of obscure SST records—when one ends, he places another on the turntable without disrupting the continuity of mood. The cliques mix around, but stick pretty much to party lines. The smokers are on the porch. Most of the homosexuals are talking about going to a dance club. The graduate students discourse on French theory. Janet X went upstairs to compare guitar pedals with some guys in a band. The lushes in the kitchen shake the last drops from empty liquor bottles. Then independent filmmaker Lulu Rivers makes an entrance with her pal Blunt Bob Brubaker, the open mic poet. I've seen him a few times around town. He also had a bit part in one of Lulu's movies. A peculiar green bottle rests in the crook of his arm.

"Hey, Blunt Bob, whataya got to drink?"

"Hey, Jimmy."

Bob and Lulu are fucked up. The pupils in their eyes roll back like eerie cue balls.

"An absinthe opium tea."

"Pour me a cup."

I follow him into the kitchen, can't find a clean cup, so I dump the ashes and left over ice cube water from one on the counter. Bob pours the drink with a steady hand.

"You're gonna be hungover tomorrow, Jimmy."

"Thanks for the heads up, Eddie. Mmm. That is strong stuff."

Helga leads Eddie out the door, across the lawn toward their respective apartments. They live next door to each other. Eddie picks up a piece of fallen fruit.

"Breakfast."

He seems to be holding the fruit without touching it—it levitates above his palm. I lose sight of them in the darkness as they duck under the limbs of the huge tree that lives in their yard. This special group has always lived on Campus Avenue, though Helga, the poet, moved in when the post-Dolls guitar player moved out, who moved in when she moved out to live with her previous boyfriend.

I don't know how Blunt Bob can see the cup without pupils, but I don't question as the syrupy liquid approaches the rim.

"Go slow with this."

The party goes straight downhill. Alaska and I find Shonenberg passed out in Mandy's squeaky metal frame bed. I've got my cup of opium and my girl, so we shut the door.

"Should we draw on his forehead?"

He's got a picture of his mother in a bikini in his wallet and a frequent flyer punch card from the Chee Chee Club. I replace a crumpled Alex Hamilton with an Abe Lincoln from my own wallet.

Alaska has already stripped to black bra and panties. The simple first kiss leads my head into spin cycle. My clothes pile up on Mandy's floor next to a stack of quality paperbacks. She's got Rimbaud's *Illuminations*, *Bastard Out Of Carolina* and a copy of an anthology called *Unnatural Disasters*. Her beau is out of it. He doesn't even stir as we fall onto the squeaky metal-framed bed next to him. My cock hangs limp despite the stimulation. Alaska rests her head on Shonenberg's bony ass. I kiss my way down the length of her body and pause to lick the baby hair on her thighs. Nirvana of skin pleasure. I drag my tongue at the crotch line of her panties. Digging a tunnel, working under the fence. My tongue ascertains a pool of wetness. I'm a dog lapping at a bottle of cream, but I can't push my whole head in, so I pull the panties all the way off. Mandy's beau groans. Alaska makes an MMMMM as her wet lips hydrate my passion. I stretch the lips over my face and wriggle my way inside her, once the shoulders are in, it's easy… drowning in her viscera, till my mouth kisses a lung, taking her breath at the wellspring, tasting the back of her nipples as I slink on up. My brain in her brain, my heart in her heart, my erect cock shooting gism out of her vagina from the inside, fucking her from the uterus outward, my arms in her arms, my hands in her hands, our eyes, our noses, our lips, kissing inside-out instead of outside-in, our hair, our hips, our inside-out love story, our tears, our years, our sexually transmitted diseases…

I come up for another sip of the elixir. Mandy, André and Lulu loom like Scooby Doo shadows over my shoulder. I take a large sip and return to my debauch. The beau kisses Alaska's mouth as I delve into her vagina. The slow rhythmic caresses of Mandy's and André's hands touch my shoulders. Alaska has flipped over now; my tongue cruises around the rim of her anus and dips into the more acidic juice of her vagina for contrast. A divine aroma. Shonenberg's cock hangs loose. He groans. Mandy and Alaska kiss the shaft of the thin purple member. Their lips fold around to kiss each other.

André's hands move into my pectoral muscles, dig in hard for a second and revert to airy dandles. Lulu dances in the corner, with cue ball eyes, clothes cast to the floor. Her huge breasts sway. One painted crimson by the party bulbs, the other dipped in the pallid glow of moonlight from the window. André has worked his way to my cock. He reaches around and plants delicate kisses on my back. His smooth boy-chest somehow naked against my skin. Time moves as if in a strobe light. Mandy and Alaska swallow the head of the beau's penis in turns. Mandy licks Alaska's filmy saliva with the tip of her tongue.

The backlit figure of Mr. Folds rises from the couch in the front room to put on another obscure album side.

I thought my friend Cecil had flown to Atlanta for business, but he's in the bathroom with his ex-girlfriend Mitzy. He sits on the crapper. She's on her knees, his cock stuffed into her mouth. Her drunken chin rests on the toilet seat. He grunts, URR. His mangy dog, the one who got kicked in the head by a little boy at the Martin Luther King Parade, sits obediently on her frenetic tail. He stands and wipes his ass with a fistful of white toilet paper. He leads his ex by the hand into the bedroom, the excited dog at his heels. Alaska's head bobs on the purple cock in time with the music. Cecil lays his ex on the floor. His running bet is about to pay off. The pubic hairs stand out red on her tiny freckled body. Cecil has the bowl of tahini dip and scoops with three fingers. Mandy's head bobs on the purple cock between beats of the atonal music. Alaska's eyes are closed, her head rests on the beau's stomach. Blunt Bob rubs her feet. André has me erect and firmly gripped.

"Sparky, sit. Sparky here."

Cecil coaxes his dog between his ex's legs. The dog laps the tahini like an exotic treat.

My head loops like a Spirograph. The control center calls for a drink. Everyone wants to cum simultaneously. Lulu works her own clitoris. Hips gyrate. Tits sway. Light scintillates across her torso. Mandy fumbles through an antique night table drawer at the bedside and hands a condom to Alaska, who straddles the beau, slips the rubber over the head and inserts his purple cock into her vagina. I'm not sure if I'm okay with that. Mandy hands another condom to André. He slips it on. She hands him a vial of personal lubricant, which he applies to one finger—OW—and jams into my ass.

"Sorry, Jimmy Jazz."

Mandy pulls Lulu onto the floor and tastes her lipstick. Lulu fumbles for her purse. I take another drink.

"How many cups?"

"My third."

"Your pupils are gone, man."

Lulu pulls a dental dam from her purse. Mandy lies naked on the floor, breasts sloping to either side of her body. As Lulu slips between her legs, André's cock finds its way up my ass.

I wake up naked in the branches of the backyard tree. The inert bodies of my friends scattered over the grass, locked in slumber, fallen fruit, as the morning sun sheds rebel light on the beauty of their frangible souls.

Catatonia, USA

"You know, you haven't worked in five months?"

With her blue eyes situated mere centimeters from my own, I am only able to focus on one eye at a time. The right has a brown fleck in the blue lens. I pull out my cock and wipe with the stiff cum rag we keep under the mattress.

"Five months. Wow. No, I hadn't realized. Five months?"

A psychic stroke constricts my thoughts. Five months? All this energy lay as waste these months of indolence. What should a man have to show? A handful of poetry readings? An orgy? My dad bought a house at my age, became a property owner, prided himself on a modicum of success.

There's a lifetime between the crack of the egg and the yolk hitting the pan. You may not believe that time is infinite, but you can't deny that every increment divides ever smaller increments. The headache that plagues me has reached a high-water mark in my brain. I can hear electricity arc through the regions and the hemispheres fire signals at each other. The forgotten alphabet on a Mayan codex. If dreams are electronic impulses in the brain, we should hook up the VCR to retrieve and decode.

"We lost the ability to feel. What is real?"

Maybe I'm in hospital; maybe I'm at home. It smells of burnt fuel and 2-stroke oil.

"Daddy, can you help me with this homework?"

"Why don't you work at a different school?"

"Why does the skeleton have no ears?"

I've been afraid to leave my mark on the world. I don't try. Future generations are bound to muck it up—pervert the message toward exploitation. I'd rather lower the flags of my piracy than see a fascist shit co-opt something I wrote. Grubby capitalists have stolen better rhymes to sell automobiles. People think revolution is progressive, but the language is plain—a turning. The ink spot, the blood spot, the ink spot, the blood spot. Revolution and counterrevolution. Should the poor switch places with the rich? Hell yeah, round and round the Möbius strip. People should take turns in the big houses at the beach. I'll take one someday, when I need a rest. Until then, I'll enjoy my unique brand of full-belly penury. I have all I need in books, music, in family. Alaska checked out a book on fellatio from the library and has been practicing. It's fantastic. My friends are good friends. Disavowing the power to change the world shouldn't hurt. Evolution never meant to reach toward utopia. By teaching a few kids to read, I intended to improve communication, bridge race and class, ameliorate poverty and mitigate suffering. As a poet, I could "dream better" and point to great wrongs. With luck, I could break cognitive dissonance's monopoly on the imagination.

"You can't even relate on a daily basis… I don't even think you're listening right now, Dan? Jimmy?"

"Daddy, I can't read this."

Perhaps, I live to see a beautiful young mod astride a Vespa scooter with her hair blowing in the wind or to drink a pint, or two pints, at the pub. A cache of small pleasures. Thrills, chills, magic, prizes.

"Daddy?"

Resigned to be a man of small desires and negligible accomplishment. To see a small truth, use a big lens. Sands through the hourglass, we move on to later phases of our lives. I've trafficked humiliation, watched humans suffer from afar. A hermit outside of society.

"Mommy barfed crackers out of her ears."

"The Elevens had a hit song. Their fourth album topped the charts."

I've distanced myself from corruption and contributed to suffering.

"I hate when you step on my feelings and blow up at me for leaving them lying around."

"Daddy?"

"If you don't work, what good are you?"

"You've failed at everything you've tried."

"Why don't you write something uplifting?"

"And put on a sport coat."

Can I apologize for what I've done in the name of Art? Can the preacher make amends for living as he preaches? Where's the Affirmative Action in our own home to protect you from my prejudice, insatiable urges and incredulous whimsy?

"Can I go to the bathroom?"

"Can you break a hundred?"

If you leave me, who will curb my desire, however small, as it cries and throws fits and manifests soft deceitful wiles?

"Mom, I miss Daddy."

"Do you have this giraffe in pink?"

"I miss him too, little Sweetheart."

Crying now, however inverted, dry tears fall like sand through a rain stick—SHHHH—and run the folds of my brain, in a helical stripe down skeleton to the stomach. I want to surprise you, be very gentle, shy, delicate, without a cross word and with my arm about your shoulders to protect you, always. Break the seal and piss tears. Father, at the end, a man who never cried, would well up when somebody remembered his mother or his dog, whenever an old song played in a commercial.

Every cruelty, every failure and every shortfall haunt every move.

"Will he come out of it?"

"It's possible."

"Is he in there?"

"I believe so."

"What does he think about all day?"

"We can't answer that scientifically. Not yet. Dolphins waft through mathematical equations under the sea and the sperm whale regales the heroes of its history. Old folks rearrange memory to live with themselves. Some remix past and present to form new realities. I don't know."

Alaska and the doctor watch the functional MRI scan of my brain on a monitor with keen interest as random lights explode and flash around the hemispheres. Actors watching tv on tv. Armagideon time on the big screen in the situation room; cities light up across the globe.

"It looks so… violent. If he comes out, when…will he be the same person?"

"Mmm. The male brain, a bit of a riddle, I'm afraid. I hate to speculate, when… if… he comes out… he may think… differently. God knows."

"We're atheists."

"Well then, no one knows."

"Daddy, Daddy…"

"Hey, kiddo, let's go to Trader Joe's and eat free samples."

The bearded store clerk offers Smart Dogs, Boca Burgers, SimulacHam, FauxFu Chops, Fat Free Lard, SubNuggets, Hokum

Bakun, Morningstar Vegetal Sausage, Eggcorns, Soya Chorizo and Stilted Chēz.

"What's with all the fake food?"

"I believe sir, that the proliferation of surrogate meat intends to wean misguided carnivores off the cow, pig and chicken habit. The oceans are empty too, you know."

"Milton called Lucifer the morning star."

"Come on, Cali, let's try the samples at Costco. After that, we can hit the farmer's market in Ocean Beach."

Caledonia stood in the cart and pointed the way ahead. Bugs Bunny as George Washington crossing the Delaware. On the way out of the store, this raven-haired beauty squeezed past us. Her business heels CLOP CLOP CLOP sounded like Clydesdale horses against the tile floor. A tight polyester skirt clung to matronly hips. She wore a prim and even proper white blouse, a super-normal work-a-day woman. Food-like items, ready-made to heat and serve, packaged in unrecyclable plastic, fill the cart.

"Hey, kiddo, why did we have you?"

"Because you didn't use a condom."

The businesswoman overheard our two-line routine and laughed out loud. She repeated the story to her partner, who laughed out loud and repeated it in the cubicle the next day and so our repartee sails across the oral tradition. *Le Bateau ivre.* We live to alter your sense of the world, breaking the social compact with tiny indiscretions at every juncture.

"Daddy."

We don't eat free samples for lunch any more. Our cupboards are full. Real vegetables from the local co-op all the way. An occasional steak cut from a cow raised up from calf by the butcher. A construction crew works on our house outside of Palo Alto. We can see the canal that cools the factory upstream. I've got a great job as a CPA in Silicon Valley. Internet commerce is on fire. A few lies on a job application will convey anyone who wants to work as far as they want to go. I stopped writing poetry. Alaska burned those nasty poems. Caledonia's on a soccer team; I'm the coach. She takes ballet on Monday, kung fu on Wednesday. On Thursdays, she helps at the homeless shelter. On Fridays, we catch a movie in the cinema. I don't watch foreign films any more—subtitles nettle my head. I haven't seen a Russ Meyer picture in two years. *Dolemite, Big Doll House, Multiple Maniacs*—I don't look for kicks in exploitation any more. ESPN shows sports all day long; I watched curling last week. It was so cool. The skip sets up the action, the bowler throws a stone and the sweeper clears a path to the goal. Caledonia goes to a private school. I don't go to poetry readings, the doctor said drunken revelry threatened my liver. I play golf weekend mornings. It relaxes me.

Alaska's happy. She has a car of her own, a powder blue Volvo. I got a good deal on it. Her breast augmentation surgery went smoothly. The bigger boobs are fun to play around with in the sack. When she isn't snowboarding, she dispenses wisdom on the Love Doctor Show on the college radio. We've got new friends. Ping pong on Wednesday nights. I don't drink at all, really, except at the company Xmas party. I can't turn down an eggnog tinctured with brandy. We're shopping for a church that can accommodate golf, soccer game days and all those weekend mountain getaways.

A PLAYLIST

The Jam - 'A' Bomb in Wardour Street

Randy Van Horne Singers - Meet the Flintstones

Circle Jerks - Deny Everything

Cockney Rejects - Oi! Oi! Oi!

Social Distortion - Ball & Chain

The Beatles - Can't Buy Me Love

John Coltrane - Giant Steps

Samhain - Initium

Patti Smith - Babelogue

Lester Bowie – B Funk

Charles Mingus - *All the Things You Could Be By Now If Sigmund Freud's Wife Was Your Mother*

Tiny Tim - Tiptoe Through the Tulips

Dusty Springfield - I Only Want to Be With You

Liz Belile - My Country, My Cunt

Woody Guthrie - The Ludlow Massacre

Angelic Upstarts - Solidarity

Aretha Franklin - Respect

Hazel Dickens - Rebel Girl

Harry McClintock - The Preacher & the Slave

Paul Robeson - Joe Hill

Billy Bragg - Which Side Are You On?

Mavis Staples - We Shall Not Be Moved

Billie Holiday - Lady Sings the Blues

PJ Harvey - To Bring You My Love

Patti Smith - The Jackson Song

Last Poets - Been Done Already

The Damned - Smash it Up

The Exploited - Let's Start a War

Cheap Trick - Surrender

Bad Religion - Fuck Armageddon… This is Hell

Dead Kennedys - We've Got a Bigger Problem Now

Martha & the Vandellas - Dancing in the Streets

Velvet Underground - Rock and Roll

R.L. Burnside - Goin' Down South

Bessie Smith - Gimme a Pigfoot

Thee Milkshakes - Red Monkey

Last Poets - On the Subway

Clarence "Frogman" Henry - Ain't Got No Home

Inch - Chicharrones

Jim Ringer - Streamlined Cannonball

The Stooges - Your Pretty Face Has Gone to Hell

The Rolling Stones - Ruby Tuesday

Johnny Thunders - Sad Vacation

Social Spit - Psycho Ward

Led Zeppelin - Stairway to Heaven

New York Dolls - Babylon

Willie Williams - Armagideon Time

A RECIPE

Vegan Mayo

1 cup avocado oil

½ cup plain, unsweetened soy milk

1 tablespoon olive oil

2 teaspoons white vinegar

½ teaspoon salt

Sometimes, this recipe fails to emulsify. Make sure your wide-mouthed mason jar is clean and at a cool room temperature.

Pour the ingredients in the jar, but slowly drizzle the avocado oil as you fluff up your mayo with an immersion blender.

Vegan mayo can be enjoyed in cabbage and crunchy vegetable coleslaw, on sandwiches or with a spoon. Make when you have a specific use in mind as it doesn't last more than a week in the fridge.

Avocado oil is delicious, but expensive. Feel free to substitute. Any light oil will probably work. And whenever aquafaba is on hand, slip it in place of the soy milk.

Original art by Michael Klam

I have written poetry, short fiction, long fiction & non-fiction. My history of DIY publishing extends to the early 90s, though my novel The Sub was published by Incommunicado Press in 1996. I was also honored to be the featured writer for City Works in 2002. I spent six years writing The Book of Books which Rich Ferguson called my "magnum opus."

I was born in 1966. I lived with my daughter's mom for 30 years before we got married on our 30th anniversary. I choose day jobs that leave me energy for writing, the best was The Museum of Death. I love books and have a home library with 3,423 volumes. I collect books from small presses like AK, Exact Change, Manic D, Black Sparrow, New Directions, City Lights & Re/Search.

I'm a veteran spoken word artist, fortunate to have shared a stage with many of my favorite writers:

Steve Abee, Linda Albertano, Dave Alvin, Don Bajema, Liz Belile, Iris Berry, Angela Boyce, Derrick Brown, Dennis Cooper, Creedle, Kimberly Dark, Sharon Elise, Maggie Estep, Raymond Federman, Rich Ferguson, Larry Fondation, reg e gaines, Weba Garretson, Pleasant Gehman, Gary Glazner, Daphne Gottlieb, Barry Graham, Cecil Hayduke, Stevie Harris, Michael Hemmingson, Stewart Home, Hank Hyena, Tamara Johnson, Shawna Kenney, Michael Klam, The Last Poets, Mary Leary, Beth Lisick, Lob, Jon Longhi, Richard Loranger, Lydia Lunch, Douglas A. Martin, Ellyn Maybe, Larry McCaffery, Jeffrey McDaniel, June Melby, Joe Milosch, minerva, Mindy Nettifee, Matthew Niblock, Alexis O'Hara, Nicole Panter, Peter Plate, Clebo Rainey, El Rivera, La Ruocco, Michelle Serros, Several Girls Galore, Shappy, Bucky Sinister, Hal Sirowitz, The Taco Shop Poets, Jervey Tervalon, Juliette Torrez, Tarin Towers, Quincy Troupe, Chris Vannoy, Lizzie Wann, Pam Ward, Ted Washington, Saul Williams, William Upski Wimsatt & The Watts Prophets. I have performed at The SDSU Avant-garde Festival, The Fringe Fest, SXSW, The National Poetry Slam & Lollapalooza 94.

www.ingramcontent.com/pod-product-compliance
Lightning Source LLC
Chambersburg PA
CBHW071425200726
48294CB00002B/524